BARBARY SLA
by Allan

AUTHOR'S NOTE

This novel is set in a time and place where harem women really were totally at the mercy of the rich men who owned them, and of the black eunuchs who supervised them. European women really were captured by the Corsairs and sold in the slave markets of the East. The Barbary States did have a reputation for treating Christian slaves unbelievably harshly, almost as animals, and there actually were slave breeding farms in the Ottoman Empire ... and although you won't find Marsa on the map, there are several places where it well could have been.

The story takes place during the long drawn out war between Britain and revolutionary and then Napoleonic France, which started in 1793 and only ended with the Battle of Waterloo twenty-two years later. Because the principal naval powers were busy fighting each other, the war gave a considerable stimulus to the Barbary Corsairs. It also saw the elimination of one of their main enemies: the Knights of Malta. Thus for much of this time, they had an almost free rein to plunder and kidnap along the coasts and islands of Southern Europe.

By this time the corsairs had replaced their sea-going galleys with fast sailing craft such as polacca-chebecs which carried a mixture of European type square sails and Arab style lanteen sails. The demand for large numbers of young male Christian galley slaves had therefore dwindled. Instead many of the Corsos, as the corsair raids were called, concentrated more on capturing young women.

In 1798, for instance, only a few years before the setting of this novel, Barbary Corsairs from Tunis carried off almost a thousand women and children from the island of San Pietro, off Sardinia. Some were ransomed a few years later, but many had disappeared, having been sold in the slave markets of North Africa and the Middle East.

Thus, although what follows is fiction, the background is realistic. However, those of a squeamish disposition are advised not to read the books of the Barbary series. For a more serious study of this fascinating period I would recommend books such as Stephen Clissold's 'The Barbary Slaves' (Elek Books), Noel Barber's 'Lords of the Golden Horn' (Macmillan), 'Harem, The World Behind the Veil' by Alev Lytle Croutier (Bloomsbury), and books about the Knights of Malta.

CHAPTER 1

THE PASHA MAKES A PURCHASE

It was in 1809 (by the Christian calendar) that the Pasha consulted me regarding the purchase of a woman - a matter which one would have thought to be a routine matter, and certainly not one in which it was either necessary or desirable to involve a renegade Englishman such as myself.

Hassan Pasha, the Governor of Marsa, was somewhat plump with a long grey beard and fierce eyes. He was much older and rather shorter than I. He wore an imposing red silk turban and a long robe, and had the commanding air of a man who had spent a lifetime in positions of authority, as indeed he had. His lips were the those of a sensuous man who enjoyed his pleasures, as again indeed he did.

Or perhaps this was accentuated that day, for we were in the cool Arab style patio of the establishment of Achmed, one of the leading slave dealers in Marsa, and women were clearly on the Pasha's mind - or perhaps just this one particular woman. He was certainly a man who knew what he wanted, and - which made me somewhat apprehensive - not one to suffer fools gladly.

"The woman I wish you to inspect," he said, "is said to be English and of aristocratic stock."

I was struck dumb at the thought of any Englishwoman, let alone one of good family, being in the hands of a Marsa slave dealer. She would certainly be a very rare and valuable item!

"And you are also English of good stock, Colonel Hussein," he continued.

"Yes, Excellency, that is so," I replied. I was still not quite used to being Colonel Hussein of the Sultan of Turkey's Janissaries, instead of merely Captain Rory Fitzgerald of His Majesty King George III's foot guards and the son of a penniless Anglo-Irish Baronet. I collected my thoughts again after the Pasha's astonishing announcement. "But of course I am now a true believer."

"May Allah be praised!"

"Indeed, Excellency," I murmured, feeling rather a fraud, for my so-called conversion to the Moslem religion had been purely for practical reasons.

"You will, I presume, be able to tell whether this woman is what Achmet says she is? It is the thought of having a real English lady in my power that appeals to me - not some strumpet, not a mere servant girl."

His eyes lit up at the thought of it. A real English lady in his harem? Yes, I could certainly see how stimulating that would be! And since she would be a Christian, enslaving her would be all the more praiseworthy.

"Yes, Excellency," I replied. "I will be able to tell and it will be a great honour to advise Your Excellency." There could be promotion in this - I was second in command of the Turkish Janissaries in Marsa under Abdul Raman Bey at that time. Or there could be disgrace. I had learnt to be careful with this autocratic individual. Anything to do with a man's harem has to be treated very seriously and is a matter of considerable delicacy.

Moreover, I wondered how much he knew of the Bey's sloth and inefficiency. But my own position as an Englishman in the employ of the Sultan was also rather uncertain, for French influence on Constantinople was strong again.

"My chief eunuch has of course examined her." The Pasha's voice cut into my thoughts. "He says she is fit and well and he is confident he can train her satisfactorily ..."

I smiled at this. I knew well the impact such training would have on a white woman. Even in my own small harem the girls were kept well trained and submissive.

"So," the Pasha continued, "if the description is genuine I shall purchase her. Otherwise Achmed shall suffer ..."

He clapped his hands and Achmed himself appeared, all bows and greasy smiles. Eager as they both were to get down to business, we must first sip tiny cups of Turkish coffee and discuss the prospects for the current Corso, or raiding season, as well as the present state of the slave market: such is the way that business is conducted in the Orient.

We might have been merchants in a London coffee house, such as I had once been familiar with, discussing the state of the markets on 'Change' - except of course that I was in the uniform of an officer of the Janissaries, with a tall white felt hat, a short blue robe, baggy Turkish shalwar breeches and yellow boots, whilst the others wore Eastern robes. And, of course, we were all speaking Arabic, sitting cross legged on large ottomans and being waited on by pretty white eunuch page boys.

Presently the dealer's Negro overseer entered the room.

He was carrying a long stiff whip with a little leash at the tip - it was the sort that was widely used to school horses and was also used by such Negroes as this to school the young women placed in their charge. He bowed to the Pasha and announced that the goods that the Pasha had returned to see were ready for his inspection in the display room.

Here, there were Eastern carpets on the floor and bright painted tiles on the walls, but the windows were barred.

"Speak to her," the Pasha said to me impatiently, indicating a heavily veiled figure standing on a low platform by one of the barred windows. What I saw was a shrinking figure on a dais, hidden behind a loose white caftan buttoned down the front. Her

4

head was covered in an all enveloping white veil through which nothing could be seen of her features.

"Speak to her in English."

The Pasha, I thought, was getting increasingly impatient to get his hands on her. It would be tactless indeed to frustrate him now that he had the bit between his teeth, as it were. He was like a man buying a horse back in Ireland. Once a horse has taken your fancy, you want quick confirmation that it is sound and well bred, and then you want to get your hands on it, try it out, ride it hard ...

Actually, the chance of a well-bred English woman becoming a slave in Barbary must be remote indeed. It was almost certain that this would turn out to be some foreign tart who had picked up a few words of English from a client.

It would, however, be considerably more tactful to tell the Pasha what he wanted to hear, and that is what I intended to do, especially as Achmed had already taken me aside and shown me a very different young woman with a pale skin, sloe eyes, flowing black hair and a well curved figure.

"Do you like this one, Effendi?" he had asked. "She is from Sardinia."

"She's not bad," I conceded. She had already been depilated but obviously not yet trained.

"Then she is yours." He had looked round to be sure we were alone, and then up at me slyly - I am taller than most, out here - "She is a virgin, unsullied. I cannot afford such a gift if the Pasha is not well pleased with the other one."

He had obviously anticipated that the Pasha would not be able to check up on what he had been told, and was rightly fearful for his sweating skin.

"Let us hope that that is the will of Allah," I had replied with a wink, "for I would not wish to be impolite towards so generous an individual as yourself!"

So now we came to the moment of truth - or perhaps, since it would not affect my reply to the Pasha, I should say of revelation.

The wrists of the woman on the dais were fastened behind her neck to a ring high up in the wall, thus keeping her upright and helpless to intervene when the buttons of her caftan were undone to allow the inspection of her body - in this way she could be freely seen and felt without interference.

The pose would also bend her slightly backwards from the waist, raising her breasts and showing them to their best advantage, like on the carved figure head at the prow of a ship.

Slave dealers always displayed their wares in the most favourable positions - especially when they were asking the sort of price Achmed would be asking for this young woman, a price I myself could certainly not even dream of affording in those days.

I moved closer to her, ready to lie in the cause of prudence and politeness. The way she shrank back showed that she could see out through the veil.

"Who are you?" I asked, in English.

"Oh thank God!" The voice, though strained, was most attractive and definitely that of an educated English lady! "Oh thank God, thank God, you're English!"

"I am," I replied. "Or, rather, Irish."

"Have you come to rescue me?"

"Impossible!" I said. All the Barbary States had signed treaties with Britain exempting, in exchange for large subsidies, British ships and subjects from capture. These treaties were often ignored, but the existence of an English slave could not be admitted officially. "I am merely here to report upon you."

"Report? Oh God, what's happening?"

The girl was almost hysterical. She started to scream out in a most unseemly fashion. "You must save me! You must! You must!"

The Negro grew angry at this sudden outburst in a language he did not understand. This was far from the submissive and humble whisper she would surely have been taught to adopt in the display room.

He raised his whip menacingly, and the effect was dramatic. Brought back to her senses, she cowered from him.

"Oh no! Don't let that brute beat me again!"

Clearly she was absolutely terrified of the Negro and his whip. I waved him back and there was a little gulp from behind the veil.

I was fascinated. I admit it. I had not heard an Englishwoman's voice for years. I was quite taken by her lilting voice and intrigued by what might be behind the veil. And what did she make of me? She would see a tall young man of military bearing, strangely dressed. Would she be impressed by the long waxed Turkish

6

moustache and short pointed beard? No wonder she had been surprised when I spoke English! But under it all I did look fairly European still. Though well burned by the sun I was still white and my hair and eyes are brown - I have been told I have humorous self-mocking eyes and a rather aristocratic Roman nose that adds to my distinguished looks.

"Tell me about yourself," I said.

"Are they going to sell me to that fat pig over there?"

It was extremely fortunate that the Pasha could not understand a word of English.

"You must be more respectful to him," I said. "Or it will be much the worse for you."

"You wouldn't abandon me to that horrible old man?"

"I have no choice," I said bitterly. "If I could buy you for myself, then I certainly would."

It was true. I had begun to wish she were mine without even seeing her face or body.

"Buy? Buy? But surely I will be ransomed?"

"Who would do that?"

"My husband!" she said. "My husband! If he can't rescue me! Wait till he hears about this!"

"I'm afraid he never will."

"Oh!" she gasped.

What did she look like? I was becoming increasingly interested - it was a long time since I had seen an English woman.

"She is indeed English, Excellency," I told the Pasha. "Beyond that, as to her breeding, it is hard to determine when I cannot read her face to know if she is lying."

I did not expect to be permitted to see the face of a woman who might be destined for the Pasha's harem. But I was wrong. The Pasha motioned to the Negro, who reached up and pulled the veil from her face.

I gave a gasp. Here was a beauty such as I had rarely seen before.

The shrewd slave dealer had had her blond hair carefully brushed straight down her back in the approved slave girl style. Blond, blue-eyed women were very much sought after in the Barbary States and sold for huge prices. This girl's hair was fine and honey coloured, like spun gold, and her eyes were a soft and alluring blue.

7

No wonder the Pasha was so taken by her - I myself was utterly overcome.

Her elfin shaped face was young and beautiful, with a straight nose and full mouth made to please a man. But it was her brilliantly blue and carefully made up eyes that really caught my attention.

She seemed to be about to burst into tears, but then she shook her head and looked boldly at me.

That is when I became obsessed with her, with owning her, with having her in my own harem, to ... yes, my loins swelled mightily for her, but of course it was mad to think of even touching her. Only one of the richest man in Marsa, such as the Pasha himself, could ever afford to buy a creature like this.

Achmed the dealer was standing in a corner, watching in silence, sensing a sale. Apart from not wishing to offend the Pasha, he had doubtless invested a large sum in purchasing her from the Rais, or Captain, of the Corso ship that had captured her, and had then spent more in having her broken in thus far, and beautified.

"Tell me about yourself," I repeated.

This time she rushed breathlessly into rapid speech - hoping, I think, to convince us she should be ransomed. I began to translate into Arabic for the Pasha.

"I am Henrietta Hamilton, wife of Captain James Hamilton of the 56th. My father is the Reverend Hubert de Vere, a cousin of Lord de Vere." The Pasha's eyes lit up at this. "He is Vicar of a village in Hampshire, and we were always the poor relations" - this I did not translate - "I fell madly in love with James. We were married quickly for his Regiment was about to sail for Malta. I have never seen him since. I followed him to Malta but his Regiment had been sent to Sicily. I love him so much. I was on my way there in a local vessel when we were attacked by a Corsair ship - oh God, oh God, what is to become of me!"

When I had translated this, I bowed low and retreated into the background. It had been an outburst that must have added considerably to the price that the Pasha was willing to pay. To enslave the wife of a Christian infidel is something that appeals greatly to the Turk. The fact that the woman still loves the husband she will never see again adds further spice to the situation, especially if she is the wife of an English officer.

8

I thought the Pasha would dismiss me now that the matter was resolved. He would not want me to speak any more with his future concubine now that her aristocratic background was established. But again I was wrong. Perhaps he was flustered, or perhaps he was pleased with my only too obvious admiration of his prize and wished to bask in it a little longer.

Achmed motioned to his Negro overseer, who came forward and started to unbutton the girl's caftan. She gasped as she tried to shake him off, but with her wrists secured to the ring bolt set in the wall behind her head she was unable to prevent those black hands remorselessly continuing down as he undid button after button.

The Negro pulled open the caftan to show off the girl's slender naked body. The Pasha's eyes were eager as he looked her up and down, then sat, leaning forward on a stool that Achmed pulled across the floor and set closely in front of her.

I too sucked in my breath, though being careful not to draw attention to myself. The body being displayed to us was indeed superb, and the twisting and writhing added to its attraction. As I had expected, she had been depilated.

At a gesture from the Pasha the Negro unfastened her chained hands from the ring bolt and turned her round so that he could admire her long slender back and soft buttocks, and then bent her forward to give him a different view of her intimacies. The girl squirmed away from every little touch despite whatever training she had had.

This was all quite normal, of course. I myself had had much less expensive girls displayed to me in a similar way before buying them. But it had been different, they had not been delicate English girls like this. My lust for this gorgeous Henrietta was rising too fast for comfort.

If only she were mine! But that could never be. It was obvious that the Pasha was about to purchase her.

CHAPTER 2 - THE SIESTA

It was the siesta hour - I stirred as I partially emerged from my sleep, and smiled as I felt a little answering tickle down between my legs and heard the rattle of a chain below the coverlet that lay over my naked body.

A warm afternoon breeze wafted through open windows covered with arabesque tracery and ornate ironwork that was intended both to keep intruders out and slave girls in.

The breeze and the high Arab style ornately carved ceilings kept the luxurious bedroom beautifully cool. The dust, noise and smells of the teeming Arab town seemed far away. The bright blue Mediterranean sky and the dry desert air of North Africa made an invigorating comparison with the seemingly interminable soft rain and mist of the Ireland of my youth, and with the damp and overcast grey skies of London and the Low Countries in which I had served as a young officer in the Guards.

I opened my eyes and yawned, looking lazily out onto the brilliant blue waters of Marsa bay where a galliot with ten oars a side was sliding swiftly out across the water, its beautiful and graceful lines something to be admired.

I recognised this craft as the one belonging to Abdul Raman Bey, the man to whom I was second in command, and who was away on a tour of inspection. Just another of his protracted holidays. Doubtless his female galley slaves were being kept well exercised in his absence.

The Bey was nominally the right hand man of Hassan Pasha, and therefore much involved in political matters, leaving me to get on with the training of the troops, which was the reason I had been sent here by the Sublime Porte in Constantinople.

Christian women used to be a rare commodity, much sort after but costly, but at that time they were readily available for small craft such as this, used by the wealthy as pleasure yachts and as a convenient method of transport across the many bays, creeks and islands in which were situated the various towns, villages and estates that made up this Turkish owned port of Marsa.

The number of captive white women being brought back to Marsa by the corsairs outnumbered the Negresses brought across the Sahara, or even the number of mulatto girls produced in the special slave breeding farms, never mind the Berber girls offered in the slave markets following a successful tribal raid.

The recent big raid on San Pietro was rather exceptional and was still boasted about, but it was quite normal for a corsair ship to return with a score or two of young white women, captured during carefully planned raids on isolated coastal farms and villages.

When would I be able to afford a galley like this? Thoughts of the girl Henrietta still plagued me and made me dissatisfied with my modest status and harem, though the girl between my legs, perhaps sensing my mood and fearing for her hide, was doing her best ...

The Bey was a General, I was only a Colonel, but far more effective and more liked by the troops.

I wriggled a little to position the tongue at my groin to better advantage, and felt the eagerness of its owner. Life was not all bad, even as a mere Colonel!

Just as maintaining a carriage with a matched team of horses had been quite a performance in London - before I had been compelled to leave so hurriedly - so too, here in Marsa, maintaining a private galley with matching teams of black and European women must, I reflected, be quite a complicated business.

In the first place there was the galliot itself. Like a finely made and beautifully finished carriage, it did not come cheap. Also, just as in London it was difficult to find an experienced coachman and a really good groom, so here it was difficult to find an experienced galley coxswain to skipper the craft and a really good whipmaster for the slaves.

Coxswains were usually Arabs, but the best whipmasters were black - just as the best overseers in farms and factories employing female slaves were also Negroes. They got much more work out of the women in their charge, particularly if the women were white, simply because they were terrified of these ugly uneducated brutes. It was the same in the harems, where black eunuchs were always used.

Marsa had one advantage over London - there, a well trained matching team of four horses with a spare could cost a fortune. But here a team of twenty-two young women - one for each oar and a couple of spares - was relatively cheap, even if half of them were white skinned, for the long drawn out war in Europe had allowed the corsairs to raid the coasts of Europe almost with impunity. Nor was the cost of feed very high, provided the whipmaster was economical. And the hard life kept them fit and well and ready at any time for use in their Master's harem if required.

I was now well aroused, and down there the girl's tongue and mouth were working hard, as the metallic clinking of a chain testified. I recognised it as coming from the heavy lower chain. One end would be fastened to the stout ring cemented into the floor at the foot of my large couch and the other to the ring at the back of the collar of whatever girl Matrak had put there.

Matrak was my chief black eunuch, and a valuable servant. I could leave the running of my small harem entirely to him whilst I got on with drilling my Janissaries.

The Pasha did well out of hiring well disciplined detachments of Janissaries, each under the command of their Agha, to the merchants who funded and fitted out ships for the Corso. My task therefore was an important one, which was why I, with my British military background, had been sent here.

Officially, of course, the Sultan disapproved of the Barbary corsairs. None were based here in Marsa, the one North African port still under his direct rule. It was strategically situated halfway between Tripoli and Tunis, with easy access to the caravan routes to the interior and across the Sahara. The stability of Marsa, with its well organised slave and grain markets, and its wealthy merchants and entrepreneurs, made it an ideal port for the corsairs to sell captured cargoes and captured women and boys. They could also seek further funding for their next Corso - and hire a detachment of my excellent Janissaries, who were far better trained than those stationed in Algiers, Tunis or Tripoli.

Yes, Marsa, and hence the Sultan, grew rich out of the revived fortunes of the Barbary corsairs. 'Praise be to Napoleon!', as the Pasha used to say, for he had also made life easier by putting an end to the Republic of Venice in 1797, and, a year later, to the Knights of Malta, both of whose fleets had for so long harried the corsairs.

Two years previously, Napoleon and the Tsar Alexander had met on the famous raft at Tilsit and secretly agreed to divide the world up between them. This had been followed by the French occupation of Spain and Portugal and by the defection of Austria. Meanwhile Napoleon's dashing cavalry commander, Marshal Murat, married to his sister Caroline, had become King of Naples, and had driven off English attempts to invade from Sicily where the Bourbon Kind Ferdinand had fled. Now there were rumours that the English troops were leaving Sicily for Spain, and that Murat was planning to invade Sicily.

I stretched out on my back with my legs apart and my hands behind my head on the soft pillows of the couch, and snapped my fingers. Immediately the soft little wet tongue was joined by the tips of delicate fingers.

I could feel the girl struggling to get higher so that she could show me her face, but the short chain is intended to prevent just that. A man did not want to be bothered with a girl's identity during his siesta - he just wanted to feel her gently pleasing him. If he desired more active sport he could always ring for another girl, one on a long chain.

From under the coverlet came the distinctive tinkling of the girl's belled slave bracelets, riveted round her wrists, as she brought the tips of her fingers more actively into play. These bracelets were not only an ornament - they also warned the black eunuchs if a girl was seeking to satisfy herself or her friends..

It was all very efficient. I was lucky to have such an experienced and effective a chief black eunuch as Matrak. I had inherited him from my predecessor when he was recalled to Constantinople.

"Leave Matrak to run your harem," I had been advised.

"I have no harem," I had protested.

"Then the sooner you get one together the better. You must have one if you want to enjoy the respect of the troops and of the local community. Leave it all to Matrak. He'll buy well and train well."

And he had!

The hidden girl was doing extremely well. I would have to congratulate Matrak, and then perhaps he would reward her with a little piece of what is called Turkish Delight in London.

London!

That seemed a long time ago! My present life was a different world altogether from my days on Guard Duty at St. James' Palace, with the evenings spent flirting with the vivacious and encouraging ladies of the Court.

I had been a lusty fellow - still was - still am, indeed - but what a fool also. I, Captain Rory Fitzgerald, the penniless son of an Irish Baronet, had been caught by the Queen herself in bed with one of her Ladies in Waiting!

To avoid a court martial, to say nothing of the scandal, the Lord Chamberlain had given me two days to get out of the country for ever. Two days! In the middle of a war!

But here I was.

The fact that I was willing to embrace the Moslem religion greatly helped my progress in the service of the Sultan. I did not take any religion very seriously and I had never been keen on the more puritanical aspects of Christianity. Certainly the Moslems seemed to have the right ideas about women.

'God has put women into the world to provide for the enjoyment of men,' says the Koran. 'Go ye, therefore, and enjoy them.' A sentiment after my own heart!

Indeed, the clinking of the chain under the covering, the exquisite tickle of the girl's tongue and of the tips of her fingers served to remind me that lustful enjoyment was the correct thing here: and of course the girls enjoyed it too.

'Man gets a glimpse of Heaven when he is in the arms of a soft, beautiful and passionate woman,' said the Prophet. May his name indeed be for ever blest, says I.

Idly I picked up the note that Matrak had left under my pillow, giving the name of the girl he had chosen for me that afternoon. I smiled as I read it: Etta!

Etta, as in Henrietta! She was the girl I had been rewarded with on that famous day. Etta sounded much better than Signorina Maria Gracia Agapacci. She was the daughter of the Mayor of a Sardinian village. When the village was raided, she had been betrothed to a young farmer. She would have been wasted as a farmer's wife, but she would make an excellent concubine.

Except - she was not Henrietta! Every time I saw her I was reminded of that fact. She was very pretty, but I simply did not long for her as I did for Henrietta.

I wondered how Henrietta was getting on. I just could not stop wondering about her life in the Pasha's harem. Every time I saw the Pasha I could not help wondering if he had just taken her. I felt so jealous and helpless. She was the only other English person in Marsa, but she was in the Pasha's harem - and not in mine!

It is, of course, a strange fact that harem life seems to make a woman genuinely want to serve and please the man who now owns

14

her, even if he is fat, repulsive and elderly. It must be the sensuous atmosphere; the utter concentration on pleasing one remote but all-powerful and dominant Master; the constant scheming to attract his attention; the deliberate denial of even the sight of any other man; the unremitting close supervision by the black eunuchs to ensure that the women do not play with themselves or each other; and the way the women thus become totally dependent on attracting their Master's attention if they are to have any relief whatsoever.

Putting a Christian girl into a harem seems to release a flood of pent-up submissiveness to the male that has been artificially held back in Europe. Perhaps they are obeying some deep primeval instinct. It is as if these beautiful creatures suddenly find themselves revelling in being the property of a rich and powerful man. Was Henrietta now revelling in being the property of the Pasha, even if she was one of perhaps thirty or more women?

The thought infuriated me. I wanted her. I needed her. She should have been mine, mine to use as I liked, as I did with Etta.

I put my hands down to adjust the position of Etta's mouth and could not resist the temptation to glance down there. All I saw was a river of long black hair and then, under it, a pair of glistening dark eyes flashing up towards me with a look of dog-like devotion.

Below her face I caught a glimpse of the carefully polished heavy brass collar that all my girls have rivetted around their necks. Her name was engraved on it, and a ring hung from the front and another from the back.

I smiled as I lowered the covering again on Etta, and she gave a little moan.

This Etta was good, but she was not Henrietta ...

Matrak would have told her that if I was satisfied with her after several performances like this, then the next step would be a long chain, the loss of her virginity and her promotion to the rank of concubine. She would have to beg for all that, humbly and submissively and in writing.

CHAPTER 3 - PLEASURE SLAVE

As I lay back during my Siesta, enjoying the attentions of Etta, I thought about how I also enjoyed receiving love letters from my slave girls.

Indeed, only that morning Matrak had handed me a particularly passionate love letter written from Francesca. She was twenty seven and before being captured had been married to a land owner on the coast south of Amalfi.

She had been given to me as a present after a particularly successful Corso, by a ship officially based in Tunis, but financed and fitted out by a consortium of Marsa merchants. It had been a detachment of my Janissaries who had led the boarding party which finally overcame the spirited defence of a well armed ship carrying a valuable cargo - and a pretty Neapolitan woman who was taking passage back to Amalfi after visiting relations in Naples.

The woman was of little interest to them, but the cargo of wool, gunpowder and seed corn had sold very well when the captured ship had been brought temporarily to Marsa - the goods were of a much higher quality than were normally available in North Africa.

The wool could be used in the local mills. Traditionally these had been staffed by Haratin slave women, the locally bred mulattos. However, as a result of the influx of European slave girls, they were now often staffed by white women under the strict supervision of Negro overseers.

Some of the wool would then be spun, woven and made into cloth for uniforms to be sold to the warring French and British forces. Some, dyed into a kaleidoscope of different colours, would be sent to the carpet factories. Here, more European girls, chained to their looms and increasingly replacing Haratin women, were trained to weave valuable carpets of various intricate designs, again under the supervision of Negro overseers.

The gunpowder, intended for the army of Napoleon, would be sold to the Rais of other corsair vessels.

The seed corn, intended to improve the yields of Calabrian farmers, would be eagerly bought by the farmers of Marsa to improve their yields for the lucrative export market to Europe and the blockading Royal Navy.

The merchants had made a profit of several hundred per cent - thanks to my Janissaries. So, knowing that my harem was still, perforce, small, they had clubbed together to give me the captured Francesca, instead of merely selling her to one of the many Marsa slave dealers.

These slave dealers played an important role in the revived economy of Marsa. Traditionally, they had mainly handled Negresses brought across the Sahara, Berber girls and their Haratin mulatto progeny, together with a smaller number of male Negro and European males. The sudden influx of large numbers of European young women and boys had changed all that.

Marsa had suddenly become the principal source of supply of young Christian girls for the whole of the Moslem world. Many of the prettiest captured girls were exported to the slave markets of Constantinople, Cairo and Damascus as well as being bought locally for the harems of the increasingly rich merchants of Marsa. To reduce a proud young Christian woman to being your humble pleasure slave was very much in keeping with the Arab and Turkish traditions of those days.

And there were many other outlets for the slave dealer's wares. Giving your teenage son a couple of white women as a birthday present, for example, had become a widespread custom.

Some merchants had even started to buy European women to be sent across the Sahara to be given to the simple, but delighted, black tribal chieftains, in exchange for the gold that was the origin of Marsa's extraordinary wealth.

European peasant girls, used to working long hours, were always in demand for the farms, carpet factories, mills, and private galleys. Arabs and Berbers regard manual work as beneath their dignity, and Negro and even Haratin women tended to be lazy. European women, however, could be make to work very well - by black overseers.

Their owners soon found that they could also obtain a useful cash bonus by having them mated to Negroes, for Haratin mulattos bred out of European women had turned out to be superior in looks and intelligence to the local breed, fathered by Arabs.

Indeed slave breeding was a busy local industry.

17

Here again, to reduce a Christian woman to the level of a brood mare much appealed to local sentiments.

It was now considered as normal to breed from a captured white skinned slave girl as it had always been to breed from a Negress slave. A swelling belly was not allowed to effect the productivity of a girl chained to her loom in mill or factory, or to her oar in a galley. As for those working on farms, they were covered annually, just as were the ewes, mares, goats and jenny donkeys.

In the Orient a swollen belly is regarded as making a young woman all the more desirable - it is what differentiates her from the rival attractions of young boys.

Thus in many harems, including my own small one, it is usual to see one or more slave girls carrying a black baby for their Master's amusement. Moreover, it is usual to keep one or more white girls in milk, for milk and yogurt are an important part of the Arab diet.

No self respecting Moslem, of course, would want his own sons to be born of a Christian woman, but to degrade her by having her covered by a Negro was simply doing the will of Allah. It was a way of getting their revenge for the way Europeans had humiliated Moslems for centuries.

In the Orient, women are kept hidden away, first by their fathers and then by their husbands. Thus women are simply not available to young men who have not yet started their own harems. But boys are!

No Arab merchant goes abroad, no Turk sets out on a campaign, no corsair sails on a cruise, without his Garzon to cook for him, to keep him company and to share his bed.

Even I had a white page boy, Tulip, although I was not seriously interested in him sexually.

The attitude of the girls to Tulip was interesting.

They bitterly resented the way he was always with me whenever I came into the harem to be entertained by them, or to witness punishment. They were also jealous of the way in which he could go out with me whilst they were kept locked up. They suspected that I used him sometimes instead of one of them. On the other hand they pitied him as a Christian slave who would never be a real man.

18

This was, of course, completely different from their attitude towards Matrak and his young assistant Abdul. They also were eunuchs, but they were burly, brutal and black.

Black harem eunuchs are specially chosen for their repulsive ugliness. They acquire considerable skill in handling white women. They stand no nonsense from them. They regard their task as simply ensuring that their Master's women compete with each other to show their adoration of him and to give him pleasure - even if he is old enough to be the girls' grandfather.

They make their task easier by stimulating the natural jealousy of the women in their charge; by preventing them from seeing any man other than their Master; by keeping them frustrated - any girl caught playing with herself or another girl is treated as if she had been unfaithful to her Master, a very grave matter indeed; by humiliatingly and relentlessly supervising and training them in the most intimate way; and, finally and most importantly, by instilling a constant fear of the cane.

They carry canes as a symbol of their authority and use them at the slightest sign of impertinence or recalcitrance. They do not use them in a wild way, but rather in a slow and drawn-out fashion in front of all the women. From the pleasure some (such as Matrak) clearly derive from flogging white women, one might imagine they are seeking revenge for all the wrongs that the white race has inflicted upon the black race in the past.

Certainly my girls were scared stiff of Matrak and young Abdul.

They were constantly whispering to each other about how angry their beloved Master would be if only he knew how cruel Matrak and Abdul were. Little did they know that he already knew and thoroughly approved!

I enjoyed listening to them and watching them unobserved through the lattice screens that looked down into the harem, even into the harem bathroom and the slave girls' dormitory.

It was always a highly satisfactory sight to look down through the lattice screen onto these pretty little creatures and to realise that they existed merely for one's private amusement and pleasures. A rich Englishman might feel the same way when contemplating his collection of Italian paintings or his stable of race horses!

There was, of course, one exception to the girls all proudly and prominently carrying my brand mark on their naked and thrusting

19

bellies. It was the Pasha's well known green brand that Carmen carried prominently on her soft white belly.

It had been a great surprise to suddenly find her one day in my harem!

With her had come a note from the Pasha saying he was sending me this Spanish girl as a present and that he suggested that I should enhance my growing reputation as a loyal Moslem by having this Christian woman mated and made into a milk slave.

He had, of course, himself taken her virginity and his black eunuchs had trained her as a pleasure slave. It is an old tradition in the Moslem world for a wealthy ruler to pass on some of his concubines to his henchmen as a gesture of his particular favour, and as a way of binding them to him. In this case, not only was the Pasha showing his satisfaction with my services by presenting me with a beautiful woman, and thereby binding me closer to him, but he was also giving me a chance of publicly dispelling any residual suspicion in Marsa that I retained a soft spot for my former fellow Christians.

Carmen had hated being the plaything of an old man, She was still in love with her young Spanish betrothed. Much to the Pasha's delight she had fought fiercely, if unavailingly, to protect her virginity. She had assumed that as I was European I would set her free. She was horrified when I told her that there was no question of my freeing her. She was far too beautiful for that! In any case, I told her, it would be an insult to the Pasha who had given her to me as a present - and a valuable one at that, for he must have paid a high price for such a well bred young woman. She would simply have to settle down and accept her new life as one of the concubines of a Turkish Colonel!

Not very surprisingly, she had at first hated being shut up in my harem. She had fought bitterly when I had immediately tried her out on the short chain. I had to send for Tulip and tell him to pull back the bottom of the bedclothes, and apply the cane to the soft buttocks he had exposed, before I was able to feel her now eager tongue at work.

The Pasha had suggested that she be mated and brought into milk. Of course a suggestion from him was as good as a command.

Horrified, when she learned of this, she assumed that at least I would be the father of her child. The truth came as a terrible shock!

Her breasts had been rather small, as is often the case with well bred European girls. Matrak therefore recommended that, since she had good child bearing hips, she should be mated with one of the Pasha's giant Dinka bodyguards.

Not only would this be a compliment to the Pasha, but it would ensure that her breasts became full and heavy so that she would, in theory, be able to feed the exceptionally large little mulatto slave, or hopefully slaves, that were growing inside her.

Carmen had fought fiercely when the day came for her to be mated. Matrak had assured me that she was now ready to conceive. With all his experience he was usually right about such matters. I had invited the Pasha, some leading Arab merchants, and several of my officers to witness the event. They would all see, just as the Pasha had suggested, that I was now a true Moslem and treated European slaves as cruelly as they did.

It had been a pleasant occasion, as we sat down in comfort, sipping our sherbet and discussing the prospects for the next Corso season, to watch the girl being got ready for her mating.

To maintain the proprieties, Matrak had put a tiny skirt, only a few inches long, round her hips, and had veiled her face. The Pasha gave a grunt of pleasure as he saw his own brand on the girl's bare belly, above the little skirt. The other guests were suitably impressed that he regarded me so highly that he had given me one of his own trained concubines.

My reputation as a strict and devout Moslem, dedicated to humbling the accursed Christians, spread far and wide.

It had all been a great success. Not only had she proved to be a capacious milk slave, but her mental attitude had also changed remarkably. The mixture of Matrak's strict harem discipline, the fear of his cane, and the realisation that there was no escape had all made her fall more and more in love with me, her cruel but wonderful Master!

It had been a remarkable example of how domination by a male brings out the inherent submissiveness of a young woman, and how she simply cannot help adoring a strong and powerful man who utterly controls her destiny ...

At the time of this story, of course, my harem was still quite small.

Apart from the three gifts, the newly enslaved Etta from Sardinia, the beautiful Carmen from Spain, and the tempestuous Francesca from Naples, there was also Marie my exquisite French girl, Paula the tall tawny haired Greek from the Ionian Islands, destined in a few months to join Carmen as a milk slave, and my two delightful young Berber girls, Lala and Muneerah.

This was, of course, a very small harem compared with those of my superior, Abdul Raman Bey, or the Pasha himself, each of whom was reputed to own twenty to thirty European girls as well as a goodly selection of Berber, Haratin and Negro ones. They also, of course, had Turkish wives.

But each of my modest number of girls was beautiful in a different way and each was passionate in an equally different way. Each reacted, too, not only differently to me but also to Matrak and his cane. It was these difference that made it so fascinating to watch them through the screens.

If only Henrietta had been there too!

My harem was just big enough to make it worth while to employ the ancillary staff that makes owning a harem so effortless as well as enjoyable: two black eunuchs and a young Italian white eunuch hairdresser.

I was just beginning to concentrate on little Etta down between my legs when there was a discreet knock at the door.

"Master! Effendi! Effendi!"

It was the piping voice of Tulip, my page boy.

He would not dare disturb me unless it was urgent.

"Come!" I called out.

CHAPTER 4 - OFF TO SEE THE PASHA

Tulip coughed discreetly, his eyes on the hump around my legs and loins.

"Your Excellency," he said in his falsetto voice, "you told me to rouse you! It is time to go to the Pasha!"

Ah yes! He was right to disturb me. I must not be late for the appointment I had requested.

With the passing of the heat of the day, the sea was now covered with various Arab craft. Some were dhows and feluccas with triangular lanteen sails set to take advantage of the evening breeze as they brought cargoes of vegetables, fish, rice, grain, slave girls and sheep from the outlying villages to the next day's market in Marsa. Others were fregatinas and dghajsas, small rowing craft carrying one or two fishermen or passengers with the rower standing up at his oars. It was a scene of considerable activity, with the female galley slaves of the Bey's twenty-oar galliot still being exercised hard.

Matrak entered. With his close set cunning eyes, his jet black skin, his thick Negroid lips and the heavy tribal scarring on his cheeks, he would have made a frightening figure even were he not so large.

He wore the bright yellow turban of a chief black eunuch, yellow barboushes on his feet, and red baggy Turkish shalwar, caught below the knees. His muscular naked torso was covered only with a short Turkish waistcoat. He carried his wand of office, a silver tipped long whippy cane which he called 'The Punisher'.

He salaamed deeply to me in the Turkish fashion and raised his eye-brows.

I nodded and he reached down silently and unlocked Etta's collar chain from the ring set in the floor and pulled the girl out backwards. She knelt abjectly on the floor on all fours, her forehead touching it between the outspread palms of her hands.

Her nudity was, if anything, accentuated by a ridiculously short frilly skirt slung around her waist. Her buttocks were nicely raised and her knees parted. Seen from behind her hairless little virgin pink beauty lips glistened entrancingly.

Nice, not Henrietta!

Again Matrak raised his eyebrows.

The fact that she was not Henrietta soured me. "Not too bad," I said. "Passable, perhaps."

I had spoken in Lingua Franca, a simple mixture of Italian, French, Greek and Arabic, which she would understand. It was the common language of the Mediterranean ports - and of harems in Marsa.

My unenthusiastic reply made Matrak scowl, and he jerked angrily on her chain. She must have realised that it meant a beating for her - at any rate, she started screaming, which naturally enraged Matrak out of all reason as he dragged her away towards the little trap door in the corner of my bedroom which led directly into the harem. It was a strict rule that a girl must only enter or leave crawling on all fours, and this door was only high enough for one to squeeze through crawling.

"Mercy, Master, mercy!" she implored, breaking loose for a moment and running towards me.

She did not get far. Matrak's threw her to the floor and his cane caught her a few times as she crawled and squealed towards the door. Then he salaamed once again and left hurriedly, his face like thunder.

I would not have liked to be Etta when Matrak got her back to the Harem! And, no doubt, she would be well to the fore on the next punishment parade.

Half an hour later, having been washed, sponged, scented and dried by Tulip, and my sharp little beard carefully perfumed, I was dressed in my blue Janissary uniform. I put on my tall white felt hat, covered with birds of paradise plumes, and threw a flowing robe over my shoulders.

As I strode down the steps of the imposing building that was the residence of the Second-in-Command of the Janissaries, I heard some very familiar little excited squeals of delight. I glanced up at a horizontal lattice slit. Nothing could be seen through it from the outside, but I knew that behind the grill my girls would be fighting to catch a glimpse of me through the window slit.

The small latticed slit was the only window in the harem that looked out onto the outside world. Normally it was kept shuttered and locked to prevent the girls from accidentally seeing other men. But every time I left Matrak would allow them a little peek, knowing that my body guards would have dutifully turned their backs to hide their faces. Sometimes as a treat he would allow them to take a peek when I returned, especially if I had been away for a few days or weeks. That was a sight that excited them even more!

Refreshed my siesta, I felt magnificent as I mounted my grey gelding, held by Tulip, who would run at my stirrup, and rode towards the gate where my escort of Janissaries were waiting. They saluted smartly with drawn sabers. Each looked immaculate, dressed like me in blue uniforms, yellow boots and tall white felt hats, our traditional uniform.

The horses looked magnificent too. It was noticeable how my strict discipline had both smartened up my men and increased their self esteem.

Originally, of course, the Janissaries, the 'jeni-chevi' or new soldiers, the world famous elite troops of the Turkish Army, had been formed from the Tribute Boys, victims of a process under which agents of the Sultan scoured the Christian provinces of Turkish Empire every four years to remove by force the most promising boys, who were then raised as Moslems and trained for the Sultan's service.

In the great days of the Ottomans Empire it had been the white hats of the Janissaries that had been the first to appear before the walls of the still Christian city of Constantinople and the last to fall back after the unsuccessful attack on Vienna two hundred years later.

The equivalent of our Regimental Colours were the brightly painted polished cauldrons in which the men cooked their pilaf. In Constantinople the Sultans learned to dread the sight of overturned cauldrons, for this was the signal for a Janissary revolt which had been the downfall of more than one Sultan. Indeed since the Janissaries had deposed the ineffective Sultan Selim two years before, and had then killed the Chief Vizier of the present Sultan, Mahmoud II, they had virtually ruled the weak Ottoman Empire.

Here in Marsa our role was to maintain the authority of the Sultan, and to provide the skilled and ruthless boarding and landing parties that were hired out to the corsairs.

To learn what was required I had embarked several times as Agha of the Janissaries in key corsair raids. The successful outcome of these had greatly enhanced my own standing with the leading Rais, many of whom were European renegades. It had also enhanced my reputation with the Moorish merchants of Marsa, who often financed the Corso. One such raid had also resulted in the acquisition of my first slave girl, the delightful French girl Marie.

My Janissaries were basically white Europeans of Balkan descent, though these days our numbers were often made up from Koulouglis, the sons of Janissaries by local women.

In the cool of the evening, we rode proudly past flat roofed houses, and on down towards the Pasha's palace through the smell and dust of the narrow streets. They were crowded with Arabs in flowing white burnous, Berbers with half veiled faces, Jews who by law had to walk barefoot through the rubbish and filth and flies that littered the streets, wealthy merchants wearing large turbans and brightly coloured robes and attended by pretty Christian page boys, haughty Albanians with long flowing moustaches and baggy Turkish shalwar breeches, muscular Negroes balancing great loads of their backs, and prosperous farmers leading donkeys laden with produce or coffles of veiled slave women, both being taken to market.

It was a scene that never failed to excite me.

CHAPTER 5 - THE PASHA IS NOT AMUSED

The Pasha greeted me in the cool white-painted patio of his sumptuous palace with a raised eyebrow - he conveyed that he was a little surprised that if the Janissaries had something of importance to say it should be the second in command who came. So far so good! I, on the other hand, was very careful to show him the due deference he deserved.

With Algiers, Tunis and Tripoli each being a virtually independent Regency and only nominally part of the Ottoman Empire, the Pasha of Marsa, the only port in North Africa still under the will of the Sultan, was an important man.

He was popular in Marsa, this large grey-bearded man who now led the way into his palace. He had presided over an economic boom. Officially Turkey might regret the upsurge of the activity of the Barbary corsairs, but in practice, under this splendid old man, Marsa had done very well out of financing them, hiring out to them my excellent Janissaries, and providing a ready market for the goods they seized and handling the young white women they captured.

Moreover, he was seen to be personally supporting the institution of female white slavery that was now such a pillar of the Marsa economy, its farms, its mills, its factories and of course its busy slave markets.

"So," he said, "where is the Bey?"

"My superior officer is on duty out of town, Excellency," I said. "He left only this morning."

"And yet you make an appointment on a matter of urgency?"

"The Bey is a fine officer, Excellency. He has been overworked lately. He thought the matter could wait his return. After all, we have only had the prisoner for a few days ..."

"What prisoner?"

I feigned reluctance. "A French slave woman, Excellency."

The Pasha stroked his beard, a habit I had noticed in him before at moments of annoyance.

"What has this to do with me?"

"I would not disagree with my superior, Excellency. Certainly not! The Bey is a fine Officer ..."

"So you said, Colonel."

"It is just that if the French are making arrangements so that their troops may land unopposed ..."

"WHAT! WHAT!"

"A landing by the French is what the prisoner speaks of, Excellency. They intend to capture North Africa, including Marsa, and doubtless throw out your Excellency, but there is no need for anxiety. The Janissaries, with Abdul Raman Bey at their head, will try to defeat them. He will be back in a few weeks. It is just that perhaps this threat is so serious that I felt you should be told immediately."

The Pasha clapped his hands and a white page boy brought in the coffee.

"Explain yourself!" he said. "Tell me everything. You have a prisoner, you say?"

"The prisoner," I said, "was the ladies maid to a certain Madame de Savoury, the wife of a Colonel de Savoury, one of the staff officers of Marshal Murat, who is now Napoleon's brother-in-law and King of Naples. She and her Mistress were sailing from Naples to Marseilles - Madame de Savoury was going back to France because of the illness of her Mother. To avoid attracting attention they were both travelling as peasant girls going with several others to work in France for the vendage, the grape harvest. The little brig they were aboard hugged the coast of Sardinia and turned into the Straits of Bonifaccio, between Corsica and Sardinia, intending to

27

run for Marseilles. Instead, they ran straight into the arms of a waiting Corsair ship from Tunis. They tried to make a run for it but of course ..."

The Pasha nodded. He knew just how fast the light corsair ships were.

They were light because they carried few guns, and they carried few guns because they did not want to pound a ship to pieces before capturing it - they wanted it and its cargo intact. Thus they relied on capturing ships by boarding them, fit work for my Janissaries with their skill at arms and their dare-devil ruthlessness.

"Unfortunately," I continued, "the maid and her Mistress were parted, and we only have the maid. When she was told by the farmer who bought her that she was to be mated, she screamed out that the French would soon come to liberate all slaves. The worried farmer brought her to the Bey."

The Pasha was stroking his beard again, but said nothing.

"She told the Bey that she had overheard much that her Mistress was told by her husband, Colonel de Savoury."

"This becomes interesting!"

"Indeed, Excellency! It seems that Napoleon has secret plans to invade North Africa, and Murat would be ideal to lead that. She says that she heard the Colonel tell his wife that Napoleon intended to turn the Mediterranean into a French lake to solve at one stroke the continual problem of providing sufficient grain for his armies and to restore French influence in the Moslem world following the failure of his invasion of Egypt nine years ago. She says that Napoleon secretly regards the Turkish Empire with contempt, but she seems to know little about how the French plan to invade North Africa."

I stopped and looked hard at the Pasha. He was obviously very disturbed.

"But," I said, "and this is what made me decide to come to see you personally. She says the French are already in touch with people in North Africa to ensure that their troops may land unopposed - Napoleon cannot spare many troops and therefore everything depends on this."

"Ah!" The Pasha was stroking his beard very hard now. "So if we could stop that ..."

"Exactly, Excellency. But the maid has no details. She does not know who the traitors are, but she is adamant that her former Mistress knows - and where the landings are planned to take place."

"Are you sure the maid cannot help us find her Mistress?"

"The Bey asked her."

"Have her sent here," said the Pasha. "Leave her with me! I'll soon get at the truth! I shall send for you again. You did well to come to me, my son."

CHAPTER 6 - THE INTERROGATION

This time the Pasha led me down a winding staircase. There was a very pungent smell, confirming that we were going to the dungeons.

Many palaces in North Africa contain dungeons for incarcerating rebels or rivals. It was also a local pastime for the rich and powerful to hold a man prisoner in their private dungeons whilst they force their attentions on his wives or favourite concubines - it is considered to add considerably to the pleasure.

This one was in fact a torture chamber with numerous instruments of torture hanging on the walls and a brazier in the corner.

In the center of the room was a trestle table. Over it was tied down my prisoner the ladies maid, a pretty young white woman, naked.

She was bent over with her feet chained wide apart, her legs slightly bent, her breasts hanging down prettily, her buttocks thrust up and her wrists and neck held in a sort of stocks. The wide planking of this prevented her from seeing behind her. A shining metal collar proclaimed her status as a slave, as did the chain linking the manacles riveted round her wrists.

Two exceptionally huge and repulsive looking Negroes stood in front of her. I recognised them as giant Dinkas, almost seven feet tall, from the Pasha's personal body guard. They were naked, except for a small breech clout. Their muscular and well oiled bodies glistened like those of Turkish wrestlers. They were exceptionally black. One was carrying a long thin black braided whip, the other a bamboo cane.

The prisoner was looking up at them in horror.

I could see the marks of the whip on her body. They seemed relatively light for such a whip. The bamboo cane, I knew, would be for the soles of her feet - the dreaded Turkish bastinado.

The Pasha walked slowly and ponderously around her, running his hand occasionally down a weal, tracing one across her buttocks and another across her back and down to her hanging breasts. It was, as I have said, a very long whip.

"She has confirmed everything you told me," he said. "But has added nothing. Yet!"

He came round to her front and pulled up her head by the hair.

"Look at me," he grunted in French.

She raised her eyes to meet his, absolutely petrified. He looked down at her for a long time. Then he let go of her hair and turned to the two whipmasters.

"No," he said slowly, making sure the girl understood, "I am not satisfied that you have told everything. You shall have another six strokes - slowly."

He held up six fingers to the giant Dinkas, who grinned cheerfully. The woman seemed to go out of her mind with fear. She was screaming and crying, words pouring out in an uncontrollable wave.

She had told everything, she kept repeating. Everything.

The Pasha turned towards me. He took me by the arm and led me out of the room and shut the door behind us, cutting off the protesting screams from the woman. He sat cross-legged on a large comfortable cushion, gesturing to me to do the same.

"I don't think you will get any more out of her," I said. "We were quite thorough when we questioned her."

"It would seem so," he agreed. "But, my son, when interrogating a woman it is advisable to break her and break her again and again. It is the only way to be sure of the real truth."

There was the sudden loud crack of a whip from behind the shut door.

"That is only the whipmaster cracking his whip in the air to frighten her." The Pasha smiled cruelly. "It will make her go tense for a few seconds. Then, as her terror subsides, and her body relaxes and goes soft, that is when the whip comes down on her."

Sure enough, now there came the whistling of the whip followed by a scream.

"My men are experts," sailed the Pasha again. "They could whip her for hours without drawing a drop of blood. It is all a question of jerking the whip back just as it falls on her skin. A fraction of a second too late and she will be half killed, but get it right and the whip winds itself painfully but relatively harmlessly around her breasts, thighs, waist or between her legs. Already terrified by the first terrible crack of the whip she will become convinced that she has been badly hurt and must confess everything."

Another loud terrifying crack, a long pause, and then the quieter sound, followed once again by an ear splitting scream.

"You cannot get facts out of a person who has been killed by the whip," said the Pasha. He had obviously studied these matters deeply, and I listened to him with great respect. "But we must make this one think she will soon be killed if the whipping goes on. The fact that she can't see behind her also helps give her the illusion of a very severe flogging, as does the way the tip of the whip catches her sensitive nipples, her soft belly and her intimacies ... did you notice, incidentally, that even working on a farm she has still been kept shorn?"

The remainder of the six strokes had now been delivered, and it sounded as if the girl was making a closer acquaintance with the whipmasters' black manhoods.

The Pasha went back into the cell and sat down on a chair right in front of the terrified and still weeping girl and motioned me to sit beside him.

I saw the marks of the latest whipping. From all the noise and screams one might well have expected to find the girl badly cut up. But, as the Pasha had explained, the whipmasters were experts at their craft and had inflicted the maximum amount of terror with a modicum of pain and no permanent harm.

"Another six strokes and you will probably die," said the Pasha.

"Yes, yes ... but I have told you all I know ..."

"Your Mistress would know more?"

"Yes, yes, she would know more, much more!"

"Describe her."

"My Mistress is handsome ...

"Go on."

"She ... she is dark ... she is twenty-eight ... of medium height ... her figure ..."

"Go on!"

"Her figure is good ..."

"We cannot find her from this! Are you ready for another six?"

"She ... she has beauty spots ...

"Ah! Go on!"

"Two moles are to the right of her beauty lips ... two on her right breasts ... may the Good Lord forgive me ..."

The Pasha turned to me in triumph.

"You see? You did not learn this!"

"It is true, Excellency. I bow before your expertise."

CHAPTER 7 - THE PASHA'S PLAN

Without another word the Pasha led me back to his private quarters. They were, of course, alongside his harem. I saw several latticed screens from which he doubtlessly amused himself by looking down, unseen, at his women.

I did not, of course, look down. A Moslem does not look at the women of another man, or discuss them.

But, by God, how I longed to do so! How I longed to try and catch a glimpse of Henrietta. It was so frustrating being so near her and yet quite unable even to ask about her.

We sat once again cross-legged on large cushions. Several strikingly pretty white page boys served us Turkish coffee and mint tea and brought us hookahs. Their lips and eyes were painted like those of harem beauties. They were, of course, captured Christian boys, now eunuchs. Like most Turks, the Pasha enjoyed using both white boys and white women, but whereas the latter were locked away in his harem, he took a pride in showing off the former.

"What will you do with the girl when you are sure she has no more to tell?" I asked.

The Pasha paused to consider this, eyes closed to help his thought. I was able to study him - the lines carved upon that cruel old face showed him to be a cunning man, and ruthless, two things which I already knew, or he would not be sitting there with his bubbling hookah.

"The farmer must be well rewarded for his acumen and commanded to silence," he said at last. "As to her, she must remain hidden. We do not want rumours of a French landing to get about, but we may need her again to identify her Mistress. If I put her into my harem the story would be all over Marsa within a day."

He paused again, then shook his head.

"She will be safer at an oar in my galley. That would be better than sending her off with your party."

"My party?"

"Listen carefully, my son." He leant forward and patted my knee affectionately. "I am the servant of our Sultan, may Allah protect him. There may be little time to save Barbary for him. Most of it may be only nominally Turkish, but at least Marsa itself is still Turkish, and he will lose it all if the French conquer us. But what proof have we for our story? The outpourings of a white slave girl, a mere ladies maid? You must remember, my Son, that French influence is strong in Constantinople. There is a French military mission there, and it was they who trained the gunners in the forts along the Dardanelles who gave such a beating to the British fleet two years ago. So the Sultan will not easily be persuaded that his friends the French are secretly planning to invade his North African territories. And anyway, there is chaos now in Constantinople with three Sultans in the past three years. No, no, we must act now, on our own initiative and with our own resources."

"You wish me to take my Janissaries north, ready to oppose the French wherever they land?"

"No! They could not succeed!"

"They are brave men, Excellency! I have trained them myself! They will die ..."

"Yes, they would die. They are far too few!"

"I was about to say they will die for you, Excellency."

"It is brains we need now, my son, not bravery. It seems the French have been secretly subverting the tribesmen. No doubt with promises of riches. Very well, we must regain their allegiance. If they turn against the French, the landing will at least be set back."

33

It was true. From what the girl had said, everything depended on an unopposed landing and the support of the tribesmen.

"Yes, Excellency," I said. "But we need to know which tribesmen are involved and get them to switch sides."

"That is so," said the Pasha. "But in any event, the tribesmen alone may not be enough to deter the French. We must also frighten them with the British Navy, and the British will want much more specific information. They suspect that we Turks are now hand in glove with the French. That is why they tried to seize our fleet in Constantinople and then to land in Egypt. Unless we have more facts they will simply suspect a ruse to divert their fleet away from somewhere else ..."

He looked at me to complete his thought.

"So," I said, "we must first find Madame de Savoury?"

"Indeed, that is the first thing you must do. Then you must take gifts to the disaffected tribesmen."

"Me? I was sent here merely to train the Janissaries," I stammered, rather excited. "Surely, the Bey ..."

"No, no! He is far too grand and lazy - and he'll tell half of Marsa all about it. You are the only Turkish official I have here whom I can trust to carry out what is required to be done with the necessary secrecy and discretion."

My God, I thought, this really could effect my career in the Turkish Service.

"But surely the tribesmen are greedy as well as fierce - the French agents will have more gold than we can match?"

"Spoken truly!"

"Horses, perhaps?"

"Do they not have horses enough already?"

"Yes, Excellency." It had been a stupid suggestion.

"Christian slave girls," he purred.

"Christian slave girls!"

"Their desire for Christian white girls, whom they can enjoy and humiliate in the name of Allah, is something they really crave and yet something we have in plenty."

It was a magnificent idea.

"You will go disguised as a slave dealer," the Pasha continued, and my mind leaped ahead.

"I will be Albanian, many slave dealers are Albanian, that will excuse my accent."

The Pasha wagged a finger in amusement.

"As I was about to say, you will go as an Albanian slave dealer. Slave dealers have taken white girls inland before, but only the dregs of the markets. You will take the most beautiful creatures that Marsa can offer, but you will keep them hidden or shrouded until it is time to make gifts to show my friendship to the men that matter, the Sheerifs and Emirs."

I had to admire the Pasha. His plan was simple and clever.

"But what will prevent them," I asked, "from accepting your presents and still siding with the French?"

"You will tell them these beautiful women are only a first consignment, a mere sample, of what will be regular three monthly deliveries - except that there is some talk of a French invasion, which, if it succeeded, would put a stop to the Corso and to all slavery!"

I could not help laughing. The idea was brilliant.

"I shall give you a large sum of money from my secret purse," he went on again. "Purchases of the women must be done discreetly over a period of several weeks. The markets are well stocked now - thanks to the summer's successful Corso. Officially you will simply be seeking to increase your own harem, and seeking fresh blood. It would be as well to talk of selling several of your existing women so as to make way for new ones. All the time you will be looking for a woman with certain moles. You can say that her younger sister is your favourite concubine and are willing to pay a high figure for the other. That is something everyone will understand. I myself have two delightful young Italian sisters in my harem."

It was true. Sisters were much sort after. He smiled and rubbed his nose, then became more serious.

"You will need a couple of reliable whipmasters and guards for the march. I shall let you have the two Dinkas you saw. I believe you already have an experienced black eunuch. Take him when you leave and perhaps send your women to lodge in my harem - No, it's alright, I won't use them - unless they are very pretty of course! And I make no promises about keeping my hands off

Carmen. Sometimes I think I was rash in giving her to you! I'm not sure that you appreciate her!"

"Your Excellency!" I protested. This talk of his harem was rubbing salt into my wounds. Would I never stop thinking of Henrietta? "Carmen is the Queen of my harem. Every time I look at her, I think of you and ask Allah to bless you for giving me such a delightful creature."

"Well ..." he smiled, mollified.

"But, in any case, Excellency, although I much appreciate your kind offer, I do have another younger black eunuch." I was not at all happy at the thought of sending my lovely young women to the Pasha's harem. It would not be long, I felt, before he had them paraded naked for his inspection. I thought it unlikely that I would get them all back, quite apart from Carmen! "I think he could adequately take charge of my harem in the absence of his superior."

"A pity," smiled the Pasha. "Well, tell him he can always consult my own chief black eunuch if he runs into any difficulties."

Then his smile turned cruel. "The combination of the two Dinkas and your black eunuch should be enough to keep your coffles trotting at a good pace."

"Coffles?" I exclaimed. "Trotting?"

"Yes, don't you see? If you put all these girls into panniers, as are normally used to transport women by camel, you will end up with a large caravan. We don't want that. No, the women will be better chained in coffles, like the Negress girls brought across the Sahara. From a distance they will seem merely another such group, and if anyone comes near you will have them drop their shrouds."

"But white women!" I objected. "They aren't strong enough!"

"Nonsense! If they are strong enough to make satisfactory galley slaves, they are strong enough to run along behind a trotting horse. Give them a month or two of hard training and your coffles will run really fast. And that will give us time to have some of the girls mated before you leave."

"What! I can't take pregnant girls trotting across the desert and up the mountains ..."

"There is only a small part of the desert to be crossed and the mountain passes are not all that high. We know that pregnant white women can pull an oar on a galley, or pull a plough, or turn a water wheel on a farm, so they can certainly run behind a trotting horse, once they have been toughened up a bit. You will make a great impression with a couple chained to your stirrup! That's the sort of thing these tribesmen like to see!"

"But why bother to have them pregnant?" I asked.

"They will be much more appreciated, I assure you. The wealth of the Emir of Tatra, for instance, comes from his cotton plantation. But his cotton grows exceptionally high. Raw black Negresses from south of the Sahara are too stupid and short to pick it properly. White women have the necessary height and intelligence, but are not strong enough. So he likes to breed from tall white women to get strong and intelligent mulattos - and you can point to those giant Dinkas of mine as the sires! Oh yes, the gifts will be much improved this way ... there is an old fort out in the country where they can be prepared. It is quite isolated with a high wall, an exercise area, dungeons you can use as mating boxes and even boilers for heating animal food."

"Animal food?"

"Of course. You can take a little meat and food for yourself and the whipmasters, but the girls will have to live on what they carry on their backs. They will be your pack animals. They will have to survive on boiled barley and a little salt, so you'll have to get their bellies adjusted, as well as training them to carry a heavy load."

I could see the Pasha had thought it all out very carefully.

"So, you have purchases to make, my son." He thrust a bag of gold coins into my hand. "But remember, we need Madame de Savoury. That is equally important. Go with my blessing and may Allah speed your quest."

CHAPTER 8 - HAREM PUNISHMENT PARADE

Clutching the Pasha's bag of gold, I rode back to my official residence, with Tulip running by my horse's head as an outward sign of my importance.

Matrak was waiting for me.

"May I parade Etta for punishment, Excellency?" he asked.

"Very good," I said. He was an admirable servant and must be encouraged. "I will beat the slut myself!"

37

I took the cane that he handed me and swished it eagerly through the air as he preceded me down the corridor and unlocked the heavy iron-studded door that led into the harem. It was, of course, also the only door out of the harem, except for the little trap door that led to my bedroom. Both were kept locked. I had noticed how my girls' eyes would constantly turn to them, no doubt dreaming of freedom or of pleasing me.

To avoid the need to open the heavy door every time the girls were fed, a special swivelling hatch had been built from the kitchen. It was too small to hold a girl trying to escape from the harem. Its design also prevented the girls from seeing the lusty young men in the kitchen as they placed the food on the swivelling shelf. No knives were allowed in the harem, of course. The girls ate with their fingers.

I strode through the big door, giving the cane another swish. It was long and whippy. Being very thin, it did not harm a girl's skin, but it certainly stung, and it certainly terrified them.

As always when I entered my harem, Tulip walked behind me in attendance, ready to run any errand, to help me off with my clothes, or even to check the state of a girl's arousal.

Lined up facing me were my six branded concubines and Etta. They were lined up in order of height with my tall Greek girl, Paula, on the right and my petite little Berber girl, Lala, on the left.

They were all wearing their formal Turkish harem dress: a little jewelled cap on their heads with a tassel hanging down the side; a stiff open embroidered bolero over the shoulders that in no way hid the charms of their breasts; coloured transparent pantaloons slung round the hip that left their bellies bare; and Turkish slippers, turned up and embroidered

The transparency of their silken pantaloons showed off their soft legs and buttocks. It also showed off their hairless beauty lips. Just as the lips of their mouths glistened under the yashmaks, so their body lips glistened under their pantaloons and their nipples glistened round the edge of their open boleros.

I stood and looked at them, enjoying the feeling of owning these magnificent creatures. Clearly Jasmine, the young Italian harem hairdresser, had been very busy. The use of a white eunuch as a hairdresser was a common exception to the rule that only black eunuchs were used in harems. Because few black women have

38

long and silky hair, black eunuchs are inexperienced as hairdressers. Effeminate white youths, particularly Italian ones, however, have a flair for beautifying women and once castrated can be safely used in a harem.

A good harem hairdresser costs a lot of money to buy - perhaps twice the price of a pretty girl. But Matrak had persuaded me that Jasmine would be a good investment and he was proved right! Jasmine had a special little alcove in the harem where he was constantly pursued by my young women, each trying to be made more glamorous than the other girls in order to catch my eye.

He could change the whole appearance of a girl from day to day by draping her long hair differently, by using belladonna to make the eyes seem huge, or by changing the way he painted her face.

In Europe, a woman exposes her shoulders to set off her jewellery. In a Turkish harem, it is the soft round belly that is left exposed - by low slung trousers. It is the sight of the belly that arouses a man here. And if the belly is nicely swollen, then so much the better. 'If you want little breasts and a flat belly,' the Turks say, 'then stick to boys!'

Just below the navel on each girl's naked belly was my green coloured brand. Here in Marsa, the black eunuchs were expert in adding a little pigment to the fresh wound of a branding, so as to make the resulting scar a bright scarlet, green or blue. On either side of the brand marks, Jasmine had cleverly painted different designs in orange-coloured henna. The effect was, of course, to draw the eyes down to the scarlet painted beauty lips, half hidden under the transparent harem trousers.

Harem trousers, and the girls' bare, softly rounded bellies, gave them all a slightly pregnant look. In fact, however, only the Greek girl, Paula, was actually so - a precaution against Carmen's milk drying up. Originally, Matrak had wanted to use Lala, my youngest girl, but I had demurred. I felt that Paula would look more erotic. Perhaps with her auburn hair she was the next best thing to the blond Henrietta.

They made a fine sight, standing as stiffly at attention as any detachment of Guardsmen, with their eyes fixed straight ahead, their hands clasped behind their necks, their heads held up high by their wide collars, and their naked bellies thrust forward over their parted legs.

How much I owed to Matrak! He would have made an excellent Drill Sergeant! In Europe, a gentleman's right hand man and confidant might be his butler, his steward or his stud groom. Here it is his chief black eunuch.

In Europe, of course, a man's whole life and domestic happiness can be spoilt by a demanding, petulant, shrewish or over-emotional wife or mistress. Here, a man's black eunuch shields him from such unpleasant matters. It is his task to cope with all the tears, jealousies, secret fears and frustration of his women, and with their minor feminine ailments. The Master does not even want to know about them. He simply wants his women to be beautiful, well trained, obedient and eager to please, though he may also delight in watching a difficult girl being broken in.

If a girl shows the slightest sign of recalcitrance in her Master's presence, then a quick word to his black eunuch, the application by him of his cane to the girl's behind, and she will think twice before behaving badly in future.

In Europe, a young woman may nag a man silly over an expensive new dress or a bracelet to show off to her woman friends. Here, it is the black eunuchs who decided how each girl is to be dressed each day and what jewellery they should wear - the girls own nothing! And if a girl particularly pleases her Master, then it is the black eunuch who trained her who is rewarded with valuable rings, not her.

Captured European women do tend to nag their Masters about being released from their slavery. But if the chief black eunuch hears the subject being raised he will lead the girl away and the sound of the swishing of a cane will be heard soon after, followed by a series of little cries. A few minutes later a very contrite and tearful young lady will be kneeling at her Master's feet, saying that she adores being his slave and begging him to keep her in his harem. So it was with me. It was certainly a wonderful system for a lusty young man!

I walked slowly down the line of young women. They stood as still as ramrods for my inspection. I pointed out the occasional not quite perfectly painted nipple or eyelid, a brass collar that had not been really well polished. Matrak noted these points down. He would deal with the culprits later.

When I reached the end of the line, Matrak gave a word of command. The girls fell to their knees and lowered their foreheads to the floor, between their outstretched fingers, their long hair flung forward over their heads. It was a position of abject obeisance. In Europe it is commonly said that no man is a god in his own home, but here in Marsa he certainly was one in his harem!

With their bottoms thrust up and shining under their diaphanous trousers, their tiny waists contrasting delightfully with their flowing hips and the long line of their backs, they made an exceptionally erotic picture. With Matrak at my side I went down the line again, this time from behind, inspecting through the girls' diaphanous harem trousers their scarlet painted beauty lips, which were outlined in black kohl like their eyes. As I passed each girl she would tremblingly try to display herself even more blatantly, perhaps seeking to catch my eye, or perhaps simply driven into doing so by seeing Matrak's cane out of the corner of her eye!

I saw that one girl, dressed in black punishment pantaloons, was trembling more than the others. It was Etta. She was sobbing with fear as the moment of her punishment approached.

I like my girls to cry. It enhances their femininity and helplessness.

Matrak gave another word of command.

Still weeping, Etta crawled forward, keeping her head to the tiled floor. Matrak read out of a large leather covered book that was kept in the harem.

"For lack of control," he intoned, "six strokes. For addressing her Master without permission, another six."

There was a hiss of surprise from the line of kneeling girls and a gasp from Etta. They had only been expecting six strokes. She now crawled to my feet. She licked my dusty boots. She had, of course, been well rehearsed by Matrak. She would also have been well washed out internally. Matrak would not risk having a terrified girl losing control of herself.

Then she raised her head and looked up at me.

"This little slave," she whispered, "deserves to be caned by her Master."

Matrak made her stand up and bend over the harem whipping table. As was intended, it was a constant reminder of the discipline under which they all lived. She reached forward and gripped the far side of the table. Her bottom was now raised by a pad under her belly. Matrak reached down and lowered her trousers. Delicately she stepped out of them.

I went up to her, and felt her. She pressed her beauty lips back into my hand. It is a secret sign of submission that Matrak teaches all my girls to do. She was already wet, the little slut! It is a curious fact that a girl who is about to be thrashed by her Master almost invariably becomes wet.

The line of kneeling girls were now facing away from me, displaying their intimacies through their transparent trousers. I could see that they too were now glistening with moisture. Such is the power of the cane over a woman. It is something in-built into a woman's mental make-up, something which she is powerless to suppress.

It was time to start Etta's punishment.

She would have been taught by Matrak that after each stroke, she would have to keep quite still until I snapped my fingers. Only then would she be able to rub her bottom or jump up and down to ease the pain. If she moved before I snapped my fingers, then the stroke would not count. So it was that when I gave her the first stroke, I saw her clench her teeth and her buttocks in a desperate attempt to keep quite still.

I snapped my fingers, and with a sob she started to rub her bottom. I could see the red weal that the cane had left. Meanwhile the other girls, still on all fours with their heads to the floor, and facing away from her, had counted aloud in unison: 'One!'

I threw the cane across the harem floor.

"Fetch!"

Etta ran across the room, taking little steps and, as she had been taught, keeping her arms swinging well away from her body and her fingers bent back. Then she knelt down and picked the cane up with her teeth. She crawled back to my feet, laid it respectfully down and begged for the second stroke.

And so it slowly continued. After six strokes, none of which, I must admit, were applied very hard, and each of which was counted aloud by the kneeling girls, I gave orders for the girls to turn round and to raise their heads slightly. They could now see each stroke, whereas before they could only hear them. I knew that each one would be secretly asking herself what it must be like to be in Etta's shoes. On the one hand she would be delighted that it was not her suffering the pain and humiliation of a harem beating - she would be resolving to do her utmost to be as obedient and submissive as possible. On the other hand, she would also perhaps be slightly regretting that she was not the one being beaten, for being beaten by a man who is sexually interested in you can be a deeply satisfying process for a woman - provided it is not too painful!

Proof of this was apparent when after the twelfth stroke I put my hand down behind Etta. Despite the pain, she was dripping wet.

Then it was all over. Etta, kneeling at my feet, tearfully looked up at me with a mixture of hatred and adoration. She thanked me for my kindness in correcting her laziness. She promised to show more zeal in future.

It was with difficulty that I resisted the temptation of have her put on a long chain there and then - and to take her virginity immediately. I was only held back by the knowledge that she would give me far greater pleasure in the end if she were kept waiting whilst Matrak completed her physical and mental training. It is like riding a horse for pleasure before it has been properly schooled by its groom. You risk a disappointing ride and perhaps spoiling all the groom's hard work.

Instead I sat down on the large Turkish sofa that was reserved for my exclusive use. I snapped my fingers. With delighted little squeals, my girls all ran eagerly to me. Lala and Muneerah sat on my knees and entwined their arms round my neck, whispering girlish endearments into my ears. Marie and Francesca knelt on all fours at my feet, looking adoringly up at me, and running their hands mischievously up my legs. Soon they were joined by the now rather sore Etta.

Carmen and Paula stood behind me. Paula's breasts, like her belly, were now getting nicely swollen. Matrak was very pleased with them, assuring me that she was going to make a first class milk slave. I could feel both girls' breasts thrusting provocatively against me as they daringly thrust their hands under my robe. This was very rousing, but I knew that it was largely cupboard love. They were looking for sweets in my pockets - I made a point of having some ready, just as I did when visiting the stables.

Matrak was very strict about fattening sweets, chocolates and cakes. He liked to keep my women sleek and eager. He well knew, of course, that girls tend to long for sweets. It was all part of his system not to allow any reward except from the hand of me, their Master.

I reached into my pocket and pulled out the little box the women had been looking for. In it was a large hand made chocolate stuffed with cream. The girls could not take their eyes off it. Casually I flung it across the room. Seven pairs of heavily made-up eyes watched it fall.

None of the girls dared move.

"Carmen!" I ordered. "Fetch!"

My lovely milk slave ran happily across the big room, her heavy breasts swaying. The other girls watched her jealously. She knelt down and, as she had been taught, clasped her hands behind her back.

Then, bending forward, she picked the chocolate up with her teeth and ran back to me and dropped it into my hand. She had been careful not to suck or nibble it, much as she must have longed to do so. I did, however, allow her to lick it gently clean.

Seven pairs of eyes were now greedily fixed on my hand. Each would be desperately longing that I would give the chocolate to her.

Laughing, I slowly put it instead into my own mouth and began to chew. It was indeed delicious. The girls were all now looking at me in disbelief. There was sheer hatred in their eyes. I saw their long painted fingers tense. How they must have longed to scratch my eyes out! I was, of course, very effectively reminding them that they were all just my slaves and playthings. But equally, of course, this cruel little game gave me a feeling of enormous power over them.

I flung the chocolate back onto the floor and then released them all to fight for it like dogs fighting over a bone. In the eyes of the law, slave girls are no more than dogs anyway.

How much more enjoyable it would have been if the delicious Mrs Henrietta Hamilton were among the scrambling screaming women. It was so frustrating knowing that this lovely English woman was shut up in the Pasha's harem. He might even at that very moment be ordering his black eunuchs to get her ready for his pleasure ...

I needed to release my pent-up feelings.

I looked around at my delightful collection of half naked female beauty. I was feeling very thirsty after my exertions with the cane.

There was a simple solution.

"Matrak!" I ordered, pointing to my beautiful milk slave. "Put Carmen on a long chain and send her to wait in my bed."

I paused. Did I really want only one girl?

Francesca and Marie had deliciously soft little tongues.

"And put Francesca and Marie on a short chain," I added as I turned to leave the harem.

How I wished I could have ordered Henrietta to have been put on the short chain as well!

CHAPTER 9 - THE PIT - AND THE PROBLEMS OF SLAVE BREEDING

Matrak and I were inside the well guarded establishment of Abu Said, the biggest cattle and slave dealer in Marsa. Supposedly we were looking for fresh stock for my own harem though actually we were preparing to buy a team of white girls for our march inland.

We looked down into a pit, leaning on the waist-high rail that surrounded it. About five feet below the surface of the ground were fifteen girls. They wore wrist and ankle shackles, each with about two feet of play.

A black whipmaster, standing on a platform that jutted out over the pit, used a long carriage whip to keep the girls moving, so as to show them off to the men looking down at them.

The girls were, of course, naked. Like the occupants of the other two pits, they had only been landed the day before, having been bought by Abu Said as a job lot from a corsair ship anxious to return to its base at Tripoli, and yet also anxious to take advantage of the better prices obtainable in Marsa.

The girls had been put straight into the pits and would be kept there for a week. They would then be taken out in small groups and smartened up in the preparation room for Abu Said's display blocks. The goats would also be taken out and combed before being penned in the display hall.

The week in the pits would be something the girls would never forget for the rest of their lives. Abu Said reckoned that it was this simple idea that was responsible for him becoming the richest slave dealer in Marsa. It served, as nothing else did, to drive home to the newly captured girls that the status of a slave girl was that of a domestic animal. It thus ensured her submissiveness and docility on the display block. It was a cheap and highly effective way of breaking a woman into slavery, and thus increasing the price that could be asked for her.

At the same time, the cunning old Abu Said also used his pits to give prospective buyers a tantalising preview of both the two and four footed animals that would shortly be on offer in his market, for he dealt in donkeys, goats and sheep as well as Christian slaves. He also dealt on horses, but they did not pass through the pits!

The men looking down into the pit were a hard-bitten lot: professional buyers from the local mills and carpet factories, farmers, stewards of large estates, vendors of human and goat milk, owners of brothels and taverns, and black eunuchs in charge of private harems.

The spotless and well cut robes, burnouses and turbans of the men made a stark contrast to the nakedness of the girls below in the pit - a contrast that the girls would feel sharply and humiliatingly, just as Abu Said intended.

I was interested to see that two of the girls were clearly in foal, to use the local expression that was applied to animals like white slave girls - so as to differentiate between them and respectable Moslem ladies.

I judged that both of the girls would give birth in about two months. There would certainly be keen interest in their swollen bellies when they were exposed on the display blocks. No doubt they had expected that their state would save them from the cruel corsairs raiding their village. The truth, of course, was the very reverse. Pregnant women were sold for high prices in the Arab slave markets, where a discerning purchaser would reckon he would be buying two for the price of one!

I remembered the Pasha had told me that inland, where amongst the Berber tribes women often went unveiled, an Emir would often show off his power and wealth by having a line of chained slave girls running behind his horse, their beautifully made harnesses matching those of his horse. Often the girls' harnesses would be belled, making the passing of the Emir both a pretty sight with the girls' naked breasts bouncing together as they ran carefully in step, and a pretty sound with their carefully chosen bells jingling in time, as the sweat ran down their naked backs.

I could see that if the girls were noticeably pregnant, then the effect would be all the greater. Up to now, young black girls had been usually used for this purpose. However, if, thanks to me, the girls were white Christian ones then the aura surrounding the Emir, and hence his influence over his tribe, would be greater still.

Suddenly my thoughts were interrupted by a Negro whipmaster carrying a basket of left over food.

"Stand aside, oh my Masters," he called out. "Stand back, if you please. The animals must be fed."

As we stepped back, the Negro emptied the contents of the basket into the pit. An assortment of half eaten crusts of bread, skins of bananas, bits of meat, lumps of cold rice, and the remains of some cooked tomatoes, all fell onto the sandy floor of the pit. It was, the Negro told us, the remains of the whipmasters' last meal. I did not feel that any human being would willingly eat such refuse.

Down in the pit, the girls evidently shared my views. I saw that they were looking at the garbage with repulsion.

But they were obviously very hungry. I saw the chained small hand of a very pretty girl reach forward towards a piece of rather stale looking bread. She picked it up gingerly, wiped off the sand and thrust it eagerly into her mouth. Another girl reached slowly for a piece of bread, but it was snatched up by another girl who pushed her aside as she hesitated. Another girl snatched at a gravy-sopped wedge of meat. Another grabbed a bit of fruit.

Then in an instant, hampered by their chains, they were all scrambling like animals, twisting and shrieking as they rolled over and fought for the remaining titbits.

The watchers were laughing at the degrading spectacle. I could not help laughing too. I realised that many of the spectators had indeed specially come to watch this feeding time.

47

"This is first food they have since being put into pit," grinned the Negro as he pointed to two girls fighting over a melon skin.

Soon there was no more garbage left.

CHAPTER 10 - ANOTHER LOAD OF SLAVE GIRLS ARRIVES

I saw that a covered cart had arrived near an empty pit towards which the spectators were eagerly going.

As two Negro whipmasters climbed down from the driving platform, I realised that this was a slave cart, bringing a load of newly captured girls to the pits of Abu Said.

Because Marsa officially had nothing to do with the Barbary corsairs, pirate ships, loaded with booty and captives after a successful Corso, were not allowed to enter the harbour - even if its merchants had been largely responsible for organising and financing the Corso. Instead, they had to unload in a little creek some twenty miles along the coast, where a jetty had been specially built.

Unusually for North Africa, there was a quite good road between Marsa and the creek, and numerous carts passed along it, drawn by oxen or teams of mules, bringing the captured cargoes and slaves to the markets of Marsa. The same carts were also used to take stores to the creek - fresh food, gunpowder, and even live sheep, all to be loaded onto corsair ships fitting out for a cruise.

This particular cart carried ten girls.

Under the cover it was barred like a cage, with a hinged door at the back for loading and unloading. It also had a long heavy metal bar which was hinged at the front of the cart, ran the full length of it, and then locked into place at the rear.

The women would crawl in from the back with the bar between their manacled ankles. Thus, when the bar was locked in place, they would be secured by their ankle chains.

This arrangement, whilst providing perfect security for women who had not yet been broken in to their slavery, permitted them to sit on the floor of the cart, their backs against its sides and their ankles chained round the bar.

48

It was a strict rule of the Corso that as soon as captured women were put on board a corsair ship, then the ship's black eunuch must strip them naked and fasten wrist and ankle chains on them. This was partly to ensure that none of them were tempted to jump overboard and partly to keep them quiet and submissive down in the ship's hold. These Christian women were, of course, totally unused to being naked. Their shame and horror, and their terror of being of being seen naked by the rough corsairs, ensured their docility.

The two Negroes let down the back of the cart. One of them unlocked the long bar.

At a word of command the ten European women, blushing with shame at being naked before so many Arab men, formed up in a single line inside the cart, their legs straddling the bar. They were all facing forward, with their buttocks towards the open rear of the cart. Their knees were bent because the lowness of the cage prevented then from standing up straight.

"Eyes straight ahead!" barked the Negro. He spoke in broken Lingua Franca, like all Negroes when addressing white women in their charge, and accompanied his order with a crack of his whip. The women were too scared to risk looking over their shoulders to see what was happening.

At another word of command, the women started to move awkwardly backwards, still straddling the bar between their legs, under which lay their ankles chains. I saw that the Negro now held a heavy coffle chain in his hand. In view of what the Pasha had told me about marching my women in coffle, I was interested to see how the Negro would handle the situation. Once the women were fastened in a coffle then there was no risk of them trying to flee or to revolt, but actually putting them into the coffle must always be a potentially dangerous moment.

This coffle chain contained ten metal collars, each separated by six feet of thick chain. The Negro reached up and fastened the end collar round the neck of the woman nearest the edge of the cart.

With her eyes fixed straight ahead, she did not at first realise what was being done to her. Then with a sweep of his powerful arms, the Negro lifted the girl off the cart. Her ankle chain slipped off the end of the bar. He set the woman, or rather girl, for she looked in her young twenties, down on the ground on her knees.

She looked round nervously, deeply embarrassed at so many men eyeing her nakedness.

"One pace backwards!" roared the Negro. Obviously he had already imposed his power of command on these women. "Eyes to your front!"

Again came the crack of the whip. Again the women shuffled awkwardly backwards. He now fastened the next collar in the coffle round the neck of the next woman, and lifted her off the cart. He placed her on the ground kneeling alongside the first girl.

He continued with the remainder, and I saw the cleverness of this system was that no girl realised that she was going to be chained to a coffle until the collar was round her neck. More important, no girl was ever completely free. Either she was chained by her ankles to the bar, or by the neck to the coffle. It was all very ingenious and gave me food for thought.

The chains and manacles were, of course, mainly intended to further impress on the women that they were now helpless slaves. Clearly there was little chance of one escaping. But there is something deeply intuitive in a woman's make-up about being chained - it makes her far more submissive and obedient - and indeed many even secretly find it exciting. Curiously enough, this particularly applies to European women who are used to being much more free than Moslem women. 'Chain a Christian girl,' goes the old Turkish saying, 'and she will enjoy being your slave.'

I saw that one of the chained girls was heavily pregnant. She was crying for her lost young husband whom she would never see again.

The cart had stopped in front of a long raised animal dip, made of brick and cement and shaped like a sheep dip. It was used to make sure that all animals coming into Abu Said's marked were thoroughly disinfected so as to reduce the risk of disease in his pits, his cages, his holding pens, his preparation room and finally on his display blocks and pens.

A group of a dozen sheep were being put through the dip as I watched. They had been driven into a low vee-shaped cattle crush, made of stout wooden bars. There were also wooden bars across the top of the cattle crush. Clearly these bars were to prevent agile four-footed animals, like these sheep, from trying to jump out of the crush. The bars on the top could be raised and lowered, and since they were at present set for small animals like sheep and goats, I saw that they would also serve to make two-legged animals crawl along the crush on all fours.

The cattle crush led into a small low holding pen, also covered with wooden bars. Only a few of the sheep were still in this pen. Men carrying pointed sticks which they poked through the bars had already driven most of them up a slatted plank which led up to the edge of the raised trough.

The plank was slippery from animal wastes, hence the slats across it. It was a natural reaction, I saw, for an animal to evacuate itself as, frightened by the sight of the black water in the dip, it was driven up the slatted plank.

One sheep was swimming along the dip. I saw a Negro, halfway along it, lean forward and casually push the sheep's head under the oily-looking dark liquid for a moment.

The remainder of the sheep had climbed down another slatted plank, at the end of the trough-like dip, into another pen from which they were driven down into an empty pit - identical to the one I had just left.

Soon the last of the sheep had been dipped. Now it was the turn of the women and once again the Negroes used their pointed sticks, this time to drive the chained line of crawling women into the holding pen. They then drove the leading girl, crying and protesting, onto the slippery wastes-covered plank that led up to the black waters of the dip.

The leading girl was pushed into the trough, followed one at a time by the rest of the coffle, strung out one behind the other. The dip was very deep, and the terrified girls found that they could not stand in it. Many of them could not swim. They had to hold onto the sides of the narrow trough as best they could with their chained hands, whilst the Negroes pulled them along by their hair.

When they reached the man in the middle, each in turn was thrust under the water and held there for several seconds. Each then came to the surface again, spluttering and spitting out the foul-tasting liquid before thankfully making her way out of the dip and down into the final holding pen.

Soon, dripping and shivering, all ten were kneeling on all fours in the pen.

Their black whipmaster lifted aside a small sheep hurdle. Beyond it was a rough stone slope that lead down into another pit.

A few minutes later the coffle of newly arrived young women were crawling in the sand at the bottom of their pit. The Negro whipmaster carefully closed and locked the hurdle at the top of the only way out of the pen, and went to stand on the little platform that jutted out over the pit, a long carriage whip in his hand.

I saw the girls were looking up at us in horror. The men found it very amusing seeing Christian girls being so utterly degraded.

As the girls had been driven down into the pit, I had noticed that, like the girls in the other pits, these girls had not yet been shorn. No self respecting Turk or Arab would buy a white woman unto he had seen her unveiled beauty lips, of course. This would be attended to in Abu Said's preparation rooms, for the girls on his display blocks were always shorn.

Slave dealers were clever about how they dealt with this problem. They knew that buyers would want to be sure about the apparent colour of a girl's head of hair was her natural colour. They would therefore instruct their Negro barbers to shave the actual beauty lips, but to leave a half moon of hair across the top of their mounds. This was known as a Moustache. It also had the effect of making the now bald beauty lips themselves stand out in a pouting and erotic way.

Naturally no black eunuch in charge of the Christian girls in a man's harem, or in a brothel, factory or farm, would later allow them to keep even a vestige of body hair. He would, on the contrary, strive to give a 'little girl' look to his charges, using special waxes, creams and tweezers to ensure that the women were always soft and smooth for their Master's greater enjoyment.

If, however, a Master was tiring of a particular girl, and planning to sell her to a slave dealer, then he would instruct his eunuchs to start growing a little tuft on, say, the right hand side of the girl's mound, so that the dealer could be sure of her natural colouring.

The dreaded expression 'growing a tuft' was therefore used to describe an unhappy girl who had been earmarked for sale. The natural cruelty and jealousy of slave girls towards each other would also lead to taunts about a girl who had not recently caught her Master's eye - 'she'll soon be growing a tuft!'

Similarly, if a black eunuch was annoyed at a girl's impertinence, or if he felt she was getting above her station, he might, instead of applying the cane to her rear, tell her that he was going to recommend to the Master that 'she should start growing a little tuft', a most effective threat.

I saw, to my surprise, that one of the girls was actually standing up in the pit. With a disdainful air she was flicking the filth from her legs and arms.

Suddenly there was a crack of the whip.

"Get down, you white slut!" screamed the Negro standing on the platform. "You animal, you get down like animal! You crawl like animal!"

"That girl who stood up," said my neighbour. "Imagine her bending over in your harem for the whip. It would be a delightful sight."

I nodded in fervent agreement. I should dearly like to buy her for my harem. But my thoughts were interrupted by a whisper from Matrak.

"Think, Effendi, how well she would march in a coffle!"

Indeed, I thought, indeed. But it was time to move on and see the goods on offer elsewhere.

As I walked away, I could not help wondering whether Mrs Henrietta Hamilton had suffered the indignities of the pit. She would have made a delicious sight being put through the trough and then made to crawl round the pit. I did not think it likely, however, for it had not been Abu Said who had sold her to the Pasha.

CHAPTER 11 - MORE MERCHANDISE OF A FEMALE NATURE

An hour later I was at the waterfront establishment of Abu Hussein, the principal rival of Abu Said. He acted purely as a wholesaler and did not sell direct to the public like Abu Said. He would purchase larger lots of girls, perhaps the entire cargo from a particular corsair ship, then sort them out and sell them to smaller dealers.

Whereas Abu Said simply brought the girls to Marsa in wagons, Abu Hussein, faced with larger numbers, used specially adapted small sailing caiques. His stock was brought directly from the creek to the security of the cages in his own well guarded slave holdings on the water's edge.

Several of the smaller dealers whom he supplied specialised in particular types of women, or in meeting the needs of particular types of buyers.

Some, for instance, specialised in sturdy strong legged peasant girls used to working for long hours in the Mediterranean sun. They were usually sold as beasts of burden to local farmers. Two types of domesticated animals were kept by Marsa farmers and market gardeners, the local breed of donkey and white slave girls or their mulatto progeny. Both cost about the same to buy, and to house and feed. Both could be harnessed to the heavy mill wheels used for grinding wheat into flour. Both could be harnessed to plough or harrow. Both could be used to turn the big wheels that raised water from the wells and sent it running along the irrigation channels.

Such girls would be used to labour under the whip of a Negro overseer by day, who would then be allowed to use them for his pleasure at night. As I have already mentioned, it had become traditional to augment farm income by breeding each year from both the Jenny, female, donkeys and from white girls who shared the donkeys' work.

Other retailers might specialise in buxom young women who were pregnant when captured. These Young Widows, as they were called, with their swelling bellies as proof of their fertility, were in widespread demand as future milk slaves in harems and brothels.

Some dealers specialised in providing intelligent looking girls who might make diligent workers in the carpet factories and cotton mills.

Others provided exotic creatures, twin sisters, mothers and daughters, or even young brothers and sisters, for the harems of jaded elderly rich Moors.

One or two dealers specialised in handling women and girls from rich or aristocratic European families. Many rich Moors were prepared to invest large sums in such an acquisition. Not only might the girl's family be willing to pay a large ransom to get her back, but meanwhile the Moor would have the satisfaction of having an aristocratic girl in his harem, or watching her labour on his private estate. She would become an increasingly valuable investment as her owner dragged out the negotiations, demanding more and more money.

There was, of course, quite a risk attaching to investing a large sum of money in purchasing such a women. She might simply be lying about the wealth of her family, or, if she were married, her husband might lose interest and fall in love with another woman if the negotiations took too long.

It was by no means uncommon for the investor to show his contempt for Christians by accepting the ransom when he had tired of the woman but to return her pregnant by the blackest of his Negroes.

There was intense rivalry between many of these more specialist retail dealers. There was, therefore, keen competition amongst them to be invited to take a look at Abu Hussein's acquisitions whilst they were being transported to Marsa. They could then put down a deposit to reserve any girl who seemed to be a sound investment.

When Abu Hussein greeted me, he was accompanied by several men whom I recognised as leading retail slave dealers. Evidently they were the favoured few who had been invited to view this cargo during the journey from the creek. As they left, they were noting down in their pocketbooks the lot numbers of the women they might later want to buy.

Abu Said was surprised to see me, but he invited me to go on board the caique, and told his whipmaster, a huge grinning Negro, to show me the women. He was clearly keen to ingratiate himself with the Turkish authorities.

Going down to the jetty, I saw a line of ten chained naked young women being taken by some Negroes towards a shed. I wondered what was going on.

Stepping aboard, I saw that the hold of the caique had been completely converted. It now contained rows of raised benches running athwartships on each side of a central passageway.

The whipmaster began to explain.

"You see, Effendi, five women on each bench, ten to a row. Six rows. Caiques can carry sixty women. This time she bring forty.

All just captured from coast near Genoa. Lovely women from Liguria."

Indeed, I thought, the corsairs really were now getting increasingly daring. The Ligurian coast was certainly well known for the beauty of its women. But it was only a short distance from the British fleet blockading Toulon. But the corsairs knew that the British were too preoccupied with the French fleet to bother about a few corsair polacca-chebecs, especially as the same vessels had, only a few days before, brought them some much needed fresh vegetables and fruit.

I saw that ten women were fastened to the front benches, and the same number to the third and fourth benches. The ten women I saw being taken to the shed must have come from the second line of benches.

The whipmaster was still talking.

"Each place on bench has own ankle stocks." Indeed I saw that the women's chained ankles were held well back and wide apart by a simple form of wooden stocks. "And for each bench we have collar yoke."

He pointed out how this was hinged at the outboard side of each bench and opened horizontally. Each half contained matching semi-circular openings for each girl's neck, with two smaller ones for her chained wrists. Thus, when, as at present, the two halves of each plank were closed together and locked into place with a simple sliding bolt, it provided a sturdy wooden enclosure for the women's pretty little throats and held their wrists up alongside their necks.

Bearing in mind that the women were already chained by the wrist and ankles, such precautions seemed a little unnecessary. Would it not be enough simply to pass a light chain through the ankle chains, rather like the bar in the wagons I had seen at Abu Said's? The Negro must have seen my look of surprise, for he immediately explained.

"Very important girls well displayed for guests during journey from creek. Plank of yoke very thick - hold up heads nicely. And plank very wide - stop girls looking down at bodies during inspections. And ankle stocks pull ankles nicely back - make girl sit well forward on edge of bench with legs well apart. So girls sitting quite still with breasts and bellies thrust forward - good position for inspecting, no?"

I nodded in agreement as I looked down the line of naked women fastened to the front bench. They were indeed beautifully displayed. I saw several of them blush under my gaze. I also saw that a number had been painted on each forehead - evidently the lot number for sales purposes.

The benches had been sited well apart in the well lit hold, so that there would be plenty of room for Abu Hussein's guests to pass between and examine each girl, as she was held rigidly still. Moreover, as the benches were well raised, it would not be necessary to bend down to inspect each girl - their naked bellies were level with my eyes.

The large ventilation slats on either side of the caique, above the benches, were too high for the chained down girls to see through. They would have no idea where they were being taken to. Keeping a slave girl in ignorance of her whereabouts, or fate, was considered in Marsa to be part of their normal control and management. It also helped to impress on the girl that she is now merely a slave.

Curiosity is not considered becoming in a slave.

If a slave girl in a harem, farm or factory starts asking questions, then she will quickly learn from her black overseer's whip that such matters are not for her to discuss. Her role is simply to serve her Master abjectly and unquestioningly.

"Effendi inspect?" asked the Negro. I nodded. It would be impolite to Abu Hussein not to do so - and anyway I was now in the market.

"Keep silence!" roared the Negro as I started to have a closer look at the displayed women. "Eyes straight ahead!"

He smacked his short dog whip menacingly against one of the planks. It had a flat piece of leather at each end. It made a frightening noise. Not for nothing were such men known as whipmasters.

It is, indeed, a delightful sensation to examine a pretty woman whilst she is held quite still and unable to see what you are doing below her neck. You can watch her face but she cannot see your hands. In this case, the women did not dare to protest nor to look at me, but tried to keep their eyes looking straight ahead. The Negro, of course, was standing right behind me, noisily tapping his dog whip against the palm of his hand, whilst I felt a pretty breast or admired the smooth bald curve between a girl's legs. His mere presence was enough to ensure the complete obedience and silence of the terrified women, who, it must be remembered, had already had to submit to numerous such inspections by Abu Hussein's guests.

"Effendi, look at this one!" The Negro indicated a particularly lovely creature with long black hair. Her belly was nicely swollen.

Bending forward, the Negro ran his hands over the girl's hips. Clearly he was practised in showing off girls held in the caique. "She drop easy," he said. "You see, plenty room, nice wide hips."

He dropped his hands to the girl's knees and then ran them up the inside of her parted thighs. She tried to close them, but her ankle stocks held them apart. I saw that the bare beauty lips were plump and pouting. Across her otherwise hairless mound was the delicate outline of the moustache.

With the girl's belly thrust forward by the ankle stocks and with her legs held wide apart, he had no difficulty in parting her prettily displayed beauty lips for my touch. I was surprised to find that she was already moist. Women are such helpless creatures. They are indeed slaves to their own sensuality, and when they are chained they are all the more likely to be aroused when touched by a good-looking young male like me!

"You see, Effendi, she natural slave girl!" laughed the Negro. The girl gave a little moan of protest, but with her chin held up high above the plank fastened round her neck she could not look down to see what we were doing. Nor, with her wrists also enclosed by the same plank, could she interfere to protect her modesty.

"She drop easy," he repeated. He withdrew his hand, releasing her lips. The girl gave a sigh of relief. But her lips were still glistening, I noticed with amusement.

"And look, Effendi!" the Negro persisted, clearly anxious to make a sale. He pointed to the girl's breasts, which were well covered with little blue veins - a sure sign, in the eyes of an Arab, of a good milk slave. Then he reached up and stroked her nipples. They sprang into hardness. He pointed to the large size of the dark circle surrounding the nipples - another sign of a potentially excellent milk slave.

"This slave give plenty milk," he said knowingly.

He lifted her breasts with the palms of his hands. The contrast between their blackness and the milky white skin of the girl was most marked.

"These getting very heavy," he announced. "Effendi, you feel!"

They were indeed surprisingly heavy. They were no longer the firm pear shaped breasts of a virgin girl, but had the slightly pendulous shape of those of a mother to be - a shape that was much admired in the Moslem world. In Europe firmness is perhaps the quality most admired. Here it is size. After all, as the Turks say: 'If you want firm little breasts, then buy a boy'.

I remembered what the Pasha had said about arriving inland with several pregnant girls running at my stirrup. This one, I decided, would be ideal. I nodded to the Negro and mentioned a price. He shook his head. He had already been offered more for her. I raised my offer and handed him two gold coins. He smiled delightedly as he bent foreword to put a line through the number painted on her forehead and wrote my name across her back.

She was mine!

I told him that Matrak would take delivery of her later. The girl looked on uncomprehendingly - unaware that she had just been sold.

Suddenly I noticed that she had a black beauty spot just by her body lips. I thought of the description of Madame de Savoury. Nonchalantly I said I liked these. The Negro laughed.

"Effendi, a few months ago we have just what you want. French lady with two black spots there and two on breast."

I caught my breath.

"What happened to her?"

"Oh, she go to some small dealer."

"Do you remember which?"

He shook his head. Damnation! I tried to keep my voice casual.

"Wouldn't your sales records show us?"

"Abu Hussein not bother with records," replied the Negro. "He sell too many, just count cash, give me commission."

My heart fell to my boots. The Negro must have seen the disappointment in my face.

"All women go to smaller Marsa dealers," he said. "You go Tal Basr market, if dealer handle that woman he have record."

The Tal Basr slave market!

CHAPTER 12 - THE SLAVE MARKETS OF TAL BASR

The Tal Basr slave market was a square that had been partly roofed over. Along its sides were arched colonnades, rather like those of a typical English cathedral cloister. Inside these were lines of platforms of various heights, used by the dealers to display their wares.

No Moor will buy a girl without seeing her naked. Indeed, he will not spend his money until he, or his black eunuch, has first examined her body. But as the market at Tal Basr was a public one, the common decencies had to be observed. Each dealer brought his women to the market chained but concealed in all-enveloping black or white bakra or shrouds. Then, when he had arranged them on his platform, he removed the shrouds, leaving the girls either in just a scandalously short thin tunic of white cotton that fastened at the front, or in a loose long white robe that also opened down the front.

The women were always secured in some way and the constant rattle of chains mingled with the raucous cries of the dealers extolling the beauty, strength, submissiveness or degree of training of their wares. The twice weekly slave markets were always crowded not only with curious onlookers, and also with the black eunuchs and overseers of the wealthy merchants and owners of estates and factories, but also with quite humble small farmers and carpet manufacturers, all keen to buy new girls or sell off surplus ones.

As I entered the market I saw a farmer pulling back the shrouds covering a pair of handsome white girls to show them to a dealer.

"A fine matched pair!" he was saying. "Trained to the plough and to the water wheel."

I saw the dealer nod his head and part the girls' robes for a closer inspection.

Low platforms were used by slave dealers who preferred to display their wares standing so that the bellies and breasts of the girls were on a level with the eyes of the potential buyer - and of the casual passer-by who might well become a buyer.

Dealers specialising in similar items of merchandise would have their stalls alongside one another - just as did sellers of leather or brass goods.

I came to the booths of a line of dealers who specialised in handsome women in their thirties and forties. They were exhibited in beautifully cut long caftans. The corsairs rarely bothered to capture older women. Why indeed should they when there were so many pretty young girls? But a woman who has survived for a dozen or so years in a harem, competing against increasingly younger girls for the attentions of her Master, will inevitably have learnt a trick or two.

Not only would many men and brothel owners be interested in acquiring such a woman, but there are in Marsa certain slave training establishments where experienced older white women are used as instructresses for their young sisters. Such establishments fulfil an important role.

A man, might, for instance, buy a beautiful but intensely shy young creature. After he had taken her virginity she might prove singularly inept in the art of giving pleasure. Perhaps his own black eunuchs, the most usual trainers of white slave girls, might not be able to get through to her, relying as they did on simple fear of the cane. Such a girl might well be sent to a love school with excellent results.

I wondered if the Pasha had sent Henrietta to such a school. Somehow, I doubted if that had been necessary.

Several of the women on display were most attractive. I saw that the dealer was parting caftans to show the women's brand marks on their thighs or bellies as proof of their former ownership. I recognised several of the brands. They were those of the leading men of Marsa. But I did not feel that Madame de Savoury would have been handled by such a dealer, nor did I think that his wares would be suitable for my march inland.

Similarly, I did not stop for long in front of a stall in which a line of young women were sewing brightly coloured strips of tapestry work, using a variety of different wools. They were highly trained mill girls, demonstrating their intelligence and dexterity. They had all been work slaves in a carpet factory which had been closed down following the death of its owner. The dealer had picked the girls up cheaply. A crowd of other mill owners were admiring the work of the girls. A trained carpet weaver is a valuable commodity. The dealer was going to make a killing!

Further on, stalls of girls were being sold as potential dancing girls. A tall slim girl was being put through her paces by her Negro overseer. She wore just a little tunic. The Negro held a chain fastened to her collar. When he gave an order she knelt gracefully on one knee before two men who were passing her platform. Another word of command and she went through a display routine. First she extended one leg. All her weight was now on her toes. She thrust her breasts provocatively towards the men and then stood sideways on to them, her hands behind her neck, her body arched back, one leg held straight behind her and the other, bent at the knee, thrust forward. She was indeed beautifully displayed.

I wondered if Madame de Savoury might have been put through similar paces in this very stall, but when I mentioned beauty spots to the dealer he just looked blank.

A young woman now held my hand between her soft breasts.

"Please, please buy me, Master," she whispered urgently. "I will serve you well."

Clearly she had been taught what was expected of her as a slave girl. She looked very feminine and lovely. The brand of her former Master glittered on her thigh. Obviously slavery had brought out her latent but instinctive and primitive desire to please a man - a feeling that in Europe even a girl in love would rarely admit to, and would usually suppress as a feeling of which she is ashamed.

I felt she was just the sort of girl, now a trained and sensuous animal, an experienced pleasure slave, who would be suitable as a lead girl on one of our coffles. She would show newly enslaved girls, chained behind her on the coffle, the reality and meaning of their slavery.

"What is her price?" I asked.

After bargaining for a few minutes, she was mine. She looked at me with glowing eyes as she was put into a holding cage at the back of the platform to await collection by my servants. She was expecting to be put into my harem. How horrified she would be when she learnt the truth! Her hands were fastened again to her neck. She would remain unsatisfied. A flap was lowered over the front of the cage. From behind it came a little sob of frustration.

I smiled at that, but when I discussed my interest in women with beauty spots I also was frustrated, for there was no reaction from him.

I passed a coffle of four girls chained by the neck and kneeling in a line on a small carpet covered platform. They were beautiful and clearly newly captured. This dealer handled high quality merchandise only.

They were dressed in spotless white silk tunics with plunging necklines, which set off their highly polished iron collars. They had been carefully groomed. The tunics were sleeveless and very short. Their wrists were loosely chained behind their backs.

The first girl in the chain was extremely attractive. She would make an excellent pleasure slave. She was dark haired with startlingly white skin.

"You like this one?" asked the Negro. Going behind the platform, he reached forward and gripped her upper arms. She gave a gasp. Her arms were already chained behind her back and now he pulled them back further, thrusting her breasts out until they were straining against the thin material of her tunic. Then he shook her, making her breasts bounce.

He saw that I was still interested.

He put his hand down on the girl's waist and touched the slip knot holding the tunic closed in front.

"No! No!" she cried.

"Kneel up!" the Negro ordered harshly. He lifted her up onto her knees, her belly now level with my eyes.

Suddenly he pulled the knot. With both hands he held back the tunic, displaying the girl to me. She had lovely bare beauty lips and a delightful little moustache of hair across her mound. Her legs seemed strong enough for a march inland.

Still holding the tunic in both hands, the Negro again gripped the girl's upper arms. Looking up, I saw that her breasts looked delightfully heavy. She would make a lovely milk slave. Equally, with her belly slightly swollen with a child, she would make a fine stirrup girl, running at the side of my horse and holding an umbrella over my head.

The Negro again shook her arms, making her breasts bounce. I saw she was gritting her teeth with the shame and humiliation, but she was not crying.

The Negro put one hand down behind her back and pushed her belly forward, towards me. He was showing me what she would look like when pregnant. It was quite delightful.

He kicked her legs apart and put his hand down lower. Now the girl was having to thrust her intimacies forward for my inspection.

"She virgin. Was engaged to be married," the Negro confided. Good Moslems enjoyed enslaving a Christian girl still in love with a pig of a Christian man.

Next the Negro used his fingers from behind. The girl cringed with shame and slumped back onto her heels.

"Kneel up!" he shouted, unfastening his short whip from his belt and tapping the girl's buttocks. "Head up! Eyes to front!"

The girl was now kneeling up rigidly at attention, her legs apart, head up, eyes looking ahead. I could see the beauty lips in front of me beginning to glisten under the attention of the Negro's fingers, the little slut!

Her tunic was now hanging down behind her from her chained wrists. Her belly was beginning to move in time with the Negro's fingers. She was blushing with shame.

"Come behind," invited the Negro. I joined him behind the little platform.

"Bend forward!" he ordered. To keep her balance she had to raise her chained wrists high behind her back as she lowered her head. The Negro pointed to her glistening intimacies. He put his hand down again and raised it to his nose, covered with the girl's juices. He invited me to do the same.

"She natural slave," he grinned. "She unable control herself! She want Master's touch!"

I nodded. She would be very suitable for the long march. The Negro replaced her tunic and retied the slip knot. She knelt up again alongside her horrified companions.

I told the Negro to put her aside for me and turned to inspect one of her companions, whom I also bought. The dealer was delighted, but he had no news of a girl with black beauty spots ...

I strolled to the stall of Ali Zammit, a dealer from whom I had bought my pair of Berber girls, Muneerah and Lala. He greeted me effusively and took me to a corner of his stall, where a pretty girl was kneeling on the edge of a platform. She was naked except for a chain that ran down from the front of her collar, back between her legs and up to the hand of a Negro who was displaying her to a wealthy looking merchant. She had a little sales tuft on the side of her mound and was clearly a girl who had learnt to enjoy her slavery.

The Negro had a dog whip in his hand and was making her display her sensuality to the merchant by rubbing herself against the chain with delightful little wriggles of her belly. The chain was glistening with the signs of her arousal.

"Do you beg to be bought?" asked the merchant. I saw that he was gross and middle aged.

"Yes, Master! Oh yes!" cried the excited girl.

The merchant reached up and felt the weight of her breasts as she continued to wriggle against the chain. He said something to the Negro, who gave the girl an order. She stopped wriggling and sucked in her belly to allow the merchant's hand to feel her under the chain. The girl was quivering with excitement.

"Buy me, Master, buy me," she cried out. "I give great pleasure!"

Keeping his hand over her intimacies, the merchant began to bargain with Ali Zammit. A deal was struck, the chain unlocked from the ring on the floor, a black bakra put over the girl. It had a little opening for the chain. The merchant handed some gold to Ali Zammit, who made an entry in his sales book and handed the end of the chain to the merchant's servant.

"Take her down to the wharf and put her aboard my luzzu," ordered the merchant. Luzzus were small vessels with lanteen sails used to bring merchandise to Marsa from the outlying estates. "I have some more replacements to buy."

When the merchant had gone, Ali Zammit turned to me.

"That girl would not have been so eager to catch his attention if she had known what will happen to her when she arrives at his estate," he laughed.

"Oh?" I said inquiringly.

"That was Achmet Abdulla, a rich retired merchant. He lives now on his estate along the coast - it's rather a remote spot, but that suits his proclivities rather well!"

"What do you mean?"

Zammit looked around. Then he spoke quietly.

"He had an accident several years ago. Now he can no longer use a woman like a normal man, so instead he enjoys watching pretty white slave girls working under the whips of his Negro overseers. I don't know just what they are made to do, but he certainly seems to get through them. He has plenty of money for buying replacement girls, he's always coming back for more - not strong working girls, but delicate pleasure slaves. It's all quite mad _ but good for my business!"

He laughed.

"I remember I sold him a young woman with two little beauty spots on her lower belly and another two on her breast. They added to her price as a pleasure slave, but he paid the extra just to have her on one of his chain gangs."

I could hardly control myself. I had actually found the dealer who had handled Madame de Savoury! Moreover, I now had the name of the man who had bought her!

I could not wait to tell the Pasha.

I had forgotten all about Henrietta for once!

CHAPTER 13 - THE MISSING LADY

The coxswain, standing behind us, nodded towards the Negro drummer boy. There was a sudden warning rattle on the drum.

Then in rapid succession came six single strokes of the drum. They were matched by six quick strokes of the oars. The light galley shot forward. We were under way. The strokes of the drum slowed and, as they did so, so the pace of the oars lengthened into a steady long stroke, driving the galley quickly across the bay and up towards the coast. The Pasha and I were off in his private galley to see Achmet Abdulla - and hopefully to find Madame de Savoury.

We were sitting comfortably in the raised poop of the galley, looking down on the long narrow rowing deck. It was delightful to recline in comfort and enjoy the sight of two rows of naked young women straining at their oars, driven to ever greater effort by the threat of the coiled whip held by the Negro whipmaster. But although it would only take a couple of hours to reach the isolated estate, the Pasha could hardly contain his impatience.

"Faster, faster," he ordered.

What a magnificent old man he was, astute and fiercely loyal to the Sultan. And, as I looked down on the twenty naked young Christian women chained to the oars of the galley, I could not help also admiring the way he used his slave women and subjected them utterly to his will.

With each drum beat twenty naked women, ten on each side of the central walkway, their bodies glistening with the oil that their whipmaster had rubbed into them, pulled back on their oars in perfect time. As they did so they raised their bellies up towards their Master, displaying the bright green scar of his brand below their navels.

The Pasha and his whipmaster were experts at extracting the maximum effort from his galley slaves without making them collapse. The speed of his galley, and the period for which it could keep up a high rate of stroke, were bywords in Marsa.

I had heard that the Pasha liked to keep a supply of virgins amongst his galley slaves, so that he could amuse himself occasionally in the sumptuous little cabin below the poop deck on which we were sitting.

Madame de Savoury's maid was seated on the starboard side. She was not yet fully fit, and the whipmaster was frequently encouraging her to further efforts.

Up in the bows of the narrow craft two young women were peering out of little cages. They gripped the bars of the cage with their manacled hands. They were reserve galley slaves, instantly available to be chained to the oar of a girl who was exhausted, or whom the Negro whipmaster wanted to rest - ready, perhaps, to return to her oar for greater efforts later on.

"They are also available to be offered to Achmet Abdulla in exchange for Madame de Savoury," the Pasha said, seeing me looking at them. "I know him well. He will not refuse such an offer."

The sun was shining. Soon sweat was running down between the breasts of the toiling women. The Pasha and I, however, were sitting in the shade of an awning as we sipped cool sherbet and watched the coastline go past.

Occasionally the Pasha would order the rate of stroke to be altered to keep the women alert. Sometimes they would be rowing gently and then, moments later, at a desperately fast stroke, with the whipmaster cracking his whip to drive them on and on.

I could see the little minxes glancing up at the Pasha out of the corner of their eyes. Only by catching his attention and being promoted to his harem could they escape from the life of a galley slave. I saw several of them glancing furtively at me. They would not often see a young man.

The Pasha spoke to me at length of his fears and hopes for Marsa. I had learnt a lot by the time we rounded a rocky cape and turned into the secluded bay on which Achmet Abdulla had built his estate.

Ten minutes later, we were being led by Achmet Abdulla's servants up a beautifully kept path towards his palatial villa, set on a small hill.

We passed a stone quarry. In it half a dozen naked white women, chained together in a line, were smashing large stones with sledgehammers. A Negro overseer with a whip in his hand was walking up and down behind them. Another chain gang were being driven by their Negro overseer to pull a large square stone across the quarry on wooden rollers towards a miniature pyramid. Another chain gang were pulling a similar square shaped stone up an incline with a tackle. The incline led up towards the top of the small pyramid. Yet another gang were laboriously laying a roadway of small stones in front of the pyramid.

Watching all these activities, seated in the shaded terrace of the villa, was the gross-looking man I had seen buying the pleasure girl from Ali Zammit. He rose and greeted the Pasha effusively and invited us to join him in a cool drink as we watched his Christian slave girls toiling in the hot sun.

He must have been astonished by the sudden arrival of the Pasha of Marsa, but for over an hour the two of them simply exchanged pleasantries. The conversation gradually came round to the question of the present day market price of slave girls.

"Allah be praised, Your Excellency, the supply of captured Christian slave girls remains excellent, keeping prices down. I have had to buy new girls only recently to replace ones which were stolen from me."

"Stolen?" said the Pasha, bristling. "By whom? Why have I not heard about this?"

"I did not like to draw more attention to this isolated estate, Your Excellency. But three months ago I suffered a serious loss. Of course I keep my women and animals locked up at night. But one night Tuaregs managed to break into one cage holding a dozen women, stole them, and disappeared. I sent out a search party the following day, but they had got clean away."

I saw the Pasha stroke his beard with annoyance. He liked to think that Marsa and its immediate surroundings was an island of law and order amidst the huge sea of disorder and chaos that made up the rest of North Africa. We had not recently suffered from any incursions from the Tuaregs.

"It was a group I particularly enjoyed watching," Achmet Abdulla continued. "They were all in their thirties or late twenties - rather more mature than the young sluts I normally buy. One of them was a particularly fascinating women I'd only bought a month previously. She was a well educated French woman, who bitterly resented her slavery and had the most unusual beauty spots - I had even paid extra for her because of them!"

I looked at the Pasha, my high hopes dashed. His face was a mask.

After another half hour of small talk, the Pasha said his farewells, saying that he must press on up the coast. He promised to send some of his own guards down here permanently to protect his old friend.

Presently the galley was under way again, and the Pasha turned to me, eyes blazing. "You must set off immediately, my son," he almost spat out. "You must find her and bring her to me."

"She might be anywhere!" I remonstrated.

"No!" he replied. "The Tuaregs keep the women they capture. They breed Haratin mulattos from them and then raise and sell the progeny. I have a Tuareg page boy, the son of a tribal chieftain. His father sent him to me to be civilised. I will send him with you. He will know which are the most likely tribes to have carried out the raid, and where their grazing grounds are. You must leave at once!"

"But how about all the girls I am supposed to be buying?" I objected.

"Your black eunuch can carry on buying them in ones and twos. Your absence from Marsa will help disguise our true plan."

He called down to the Negro whipmaster on the catwalk that separated the rowing benches. "Get those sluts working harder - or I'll find a new whipmaster!"

CHAPTER 14 - THE GIRL HERD

"Go and look at the herd," Attici had said.

Attici was the Amenoukal, leader, of this particular tribe.

I had assumed that he was inviting me to go and look at their herd of sheep, whilst my servant, Zachet, the Pasha's Tuareg page boy, was pitching my tent alongside the Tuareg encampment he had led me to. But Attici's next words made my spine tingle.

"Use any of them to assuage your manly feelings after your long ride," he said. I pricked up my ears. Then he added with a laugh, "But until they have been suitably mated they must only be used as one would a boy."

Until then I had been disappointed at not seeing any white women in the encampment. There seemed a high probability that the woman I sought had been carried off by this particular tribe, for Zachet and I had heard two of them boasting of raiding an isolated estate near Marsa.

It had been a long journey to locate this tribe. I must not, I knew, disclose the real reason for my journey.

Attici was a noble of the Teghe-Mellet tribe of the Tuareg - themselves a part of the Berber people. The Berbers were a white race who had been in North Africa long before the Arabs came with their Islamic religion - a religion which sits very lightly on the Tuareg.

Berber women were not veiled, and held a position of importance in their tribe. They could, for instance, read and write, whereas many Arabs deliberately kept their women illiterate - often even their wives and daughters. Arabs felt that women should not be distracted from their main role in life - pleasing men. 'I have twenty women in my harem,' an Arab might boast, 'and not one can read or write.'

Berber women were even rumoured to take lovers quite openly, in addition to their husbands. If an Arab woman did this, she would be stoned to death.

Unlike most of the Tuareg tribes, the Teghe-Mellet made their home not in the desert itself but on its edge in the hills. They were nomadic, living off their herds of animals, which they slowly drove across the grass veld.

But, living not far from Marsa, they had also learned to take advantage of the great change that the seemingly endless war in Europe had made to Marsa's fortunes. They had adapted to Marsa becoming the entrepot port for the trade that Barbary corsairs now brought to it: the many cargoes of captured European ships, and the many white Christian female slaves they captured on the now unguarded coasts of Southern Europe.

For centuries, the Arabs in the more settled areas, and the Berber tribesmen in the oases, had used the Haratin, as they called the half Negro mulattos who the Tuaregs bred for domestic and agricultural labour. They were more docile than the pure blacks who had to be brought across the Sahara from the Soudan in slave caravans, and also more intelligent.

Some of these brown coloured Haratin were the result of a cross between black slave girls and their Berber or Arab Masters. But this was rare, since normally the children of a Moslem, irrespective of their colour, would be raised as free members of the Master's family. Most Haratin were the offspring of captured Berber women, kidnapped during the interminable inter-tribal raids, and deliberately mated with black slaves. Using captured women in this way was also a way of showing one's contempt for a rival tribe, or of showing one's domination over a conquered one.

Thus the Teghe-Mellet had for centuries bred and herded both sheep and captured women.

Now the sudden availability of large numbers of cheap white women in the slave market of Marsa had given a further boost to breeding Haratin. Naturally, no independent minded Berber woman was going to accept her husband introducing a captured white woman into her household, but they welcomed using them to breed Haratin children who could be sold for a good price.

Indeed, Attici explained, they had found that crossing their big black slaves with European women resulted in a much improved breed of Haratin.

"Go and look at our girl herd," Attici had repeated. "You will find them over the hill, being watched over by boys."

Leaving the black tents of the encampment, I had ridden across the grass and scrub in the direction he had indicated.

"Greetings in the name of Allah, the only true God," said the young boy who galloped up to me as soon as I reached the crest of the hill. Arabic was not his mother tongue, and he spoke it in a rather stilted but formal way. Clearly, however, the Berber women educated their children well.

"And of Mohammed, his prophet," I replied. I saw that a long cattle whip hung from the boy's saddle.

I looked down into the little valley. I knew that the sheep, several hundred of them, would be grazing off the sparse grass in the next valley. But here it was the women that caught my eye, spread out as they picked berries and dug for roots with their bare hands. The Tuaregs did not waste their own precious food on their herds.

"A fine herd!" I said.

"We think so," said the boy proudly, "and now they are ready for mating."

"Mating?" I asked. Sometimes I wondered if slave owners in North Africa ever thought of anything else but breeding from their slave girls.

"This is the moon of the mating. They dropped in the spring. Now they are ready for mating again."

"But what happened to their progeny?" I asked the boy. He seemed very intelligent for a young boy.

"They were Haratin. They are being raised in a secret oasis by some of our grown up Haratin slaves. We take the herd to that oasis every spring just before they are all due. Then we take the babies away from them as soon as their milk has come on well. Then we milk them every morning and evening. Their milk is of the finest."

White women's milk was considered a great delicacy by both Arabs and Tuaregs.

"They seem quiet and docile," I said. "How many do you have?"

"Seventy two," the boy replied, "including twelve that were captured in a raid three months ago."

So I was in the right place! I tried to keep the excitement out of my voice as I carried on the conversation. I must not show my interest in a particular woman.

"So you had sixty young?" I asked in a casual voice.

"Seventy one," replied the boy with a laugh. "Six had twins, and one died. Our had twins. And six of the captured ones were also pregnant."

There was nothing wrong with these Tuareg boys mental arithmetic!

"Would you like to see them close up?" he asked. "We're just about to drive them to water."

I nodded. I could not trust my voice. Was I at last about to see Madame de Savoury?

The boy put his fingers to his mouth and gave a piercing whistle, followed by a distinctive wave of his hand. He pointed to me. The two boys, on their horses across the valley, waved back.

"Hei! Hei!" they cried as they rode down towards the grazing herd. "Hei! Hei!"

Their whips cracked and the women began to run together. Clearly their young drovers knew their business. In no time, they were in a compact group. The boys rode round them, whips cracking, keeping them in a close milling mass, running round and round to avoid the whip and wondering in what direction they were to go.

"Hei! Hei!" called the young boys again, kicking their heels into the flanks of their horses on the far side of the herd and again cracking their whips.

I saw that the naked women were now moving towards me, raising a dust cloud. The two boys were on either side of them and slightly behind.

"Har! Har!" cried the boys in a more urgent voice, again accompanied by more cracking of their whips.

Suddenly, whilst one boy remained behind the women, encouraging them on with cries and much cracking of his whip, the other spurred his horse quickly round to the front, heading them off and turning them. It was expertly done. Now, not more than a few yards in front of where I sat on my horse, they were packed into a tight circle.

The boys lowered the whips and the herd became stationary, but remained compact.

"You boys certainly drive them well," I said.

"Thank you," said one of the boys who had driven them up from the valley. He too spoke excellent, if rather stilted, Arabic. "We practice it, of course. If danger should threaten, we must drive them quickly into the protection of the encampment."

"It is the same with the sheep," called out the other boy.

"Of course," I said.

These boys, and others like them, were traditionally sent out with the herds of the tribe, but to watch over them not to defend them. As the boy had said, at the first sign of danger, such as the appearance of a group of strangers who might be the advance party of raiders from another tribe, then they would run the women the mile or two back to the encampment. They would have to run very fast to avoid capture and keep together with no stragglers. Clearly they would have to be kept very fit - and instantly obedient to the orders and whips of the herd boys. Two boys would run them back to the encampment, the third boy would race ahead to give the alarm.

The group of women had considerable value, particularly after the mating season. Other tribes would be only too keen to capture them. Many of the women would themselves have been acquired in such raids, often in raids on the Arab farmers in the more settled areas - or on the large estates surrounding Marsa, such as that of Achmet Abdulla.

"It is a fine sight," I said.

The women were still a little out of breath from running so quickly up the hill. Their breasts were rising and falling from their exertion in the heat.

"We have the finest women of all the Tuaregs," said the boy next to me. "See how fit they are. These white women produce the best Haratin."

Indeed, I thought, considering how little they had to eat, it was extraordinary that they did not look half starved. But the Tuareg themselves seemed to thrive in the desert on little more: a few dates, a little ground millet mixed with water, some lamb fat, and a little salt. Such a diet makes for a tall and willowy race.

"Their hair ...?" I asked. It was along and glistening with good health, and there was a good market for genuine European hair from wig makers.

"We usually cut it in the spring," the boy explained. "We find it pays to let it grow again for two years."

Doubtless the hair they sold had made its way to Europe. Just as the Tuaregs sheared their sheep herds, so too they regarded shearing and selling the hair of captive women quite normal.

"We drive them to water twice a day," said one boy. "The water is often at a distance. This gives us a chance to practise a fast run over quite a long distance and, of course, of keeping them together. So watering keeps them both fit and disciplined - even after the mating season."

They certainly exploited their women well. What a pity, I thought, that being nomads they cannot use their labour. That, of course, is where a farming community would score. I had seen white female slaves harnessed to the water scoops at the wells, pulling ploughs, hoeing lines of vegetables and feeding animals. But, equally, such farmers risked losing them in a Tuareg raid - together with their horses, their sheep and their own women.

"Do they ever stray?" I asked.

"No!" laughed one of the boys, slapping the handle of the whip meaningfully against the palm of his hand.

"Do any try and escape?"

"No!" replied one boy.

"Well, not more than once," laughed another. "Where would they go? Where would they hide? We Tuaregs are expert trackers, and when we catch a girl who has tried to run away or get rid of her child, we hand her over to the women of the tribe for punishment. They soon make the girl realise that she must not even think about escaping her fate!"

Now that the boys' whips were lowered, the women were still standing still in a tight group. They were eyeing the boys and myself anxiously as we discussed them. None of them dared even to exchange a whisper. It was as if they had lost the ability to speak - the one attribute that distinguishes humans from animals.

I looked at them more closely. They varied in age from teenagers to women in their late thirties. They had the bodies of athletes - not very surprising in view of the way they were run and the sparse diet on which they were kept. But there was no doubt that they were sleek, fit and well.

"See what fine hips they have," said one of the boys proudly. "Since we keep them running every day right up to the moment they drop their foals, we hardly ever have problems. We do not keep any very slim hipped ones who might have trouble."

I saw that several of them had been marked with a patch of different shades of red paint, high up between their shoulders where they could not get at it.

"We have started mating the ones with the palest shade of red," explained another of the boys. "You must come and watch this evening."

"So you get a yearly crop of Haratin from all the herd?" I asked.

"Of course," came the reply. "One that proves barren is no use to us. We quickly sell her."

"Will you keep all the herd until they give birth?"

"Most of them. Sometimes the price for a pregnant white girl becomes very high in the slave markets in winter. With the corsair ships laid up for winter, the supply dries up. So then we may sell some to travelling slave dealers."

These young boys were very well informed, I thought. I remembered how in Ireland young farmers' sons would also talk knowledgeably about farm prices, and about which cows would calf next. Like these boys, they would hear their elders discussing little else.

"How will you replace those you sell?" I asked. It was a silly question!

"By raiding!" The boys all laughed. "Soon we will be old enough to go raiding too."

"Last year," said one boy, "we even recaptured one we had just sold!"

I had been asking questions politely as the boys showed off their women, but I was anxiously wondering if I would ever have a chance of seeing if Madame de Savoury was amongst them.

"Would you like to inspect them?" asked the boy who seemed to be in charge. I felt my heart give a jump as I nodded, trying not to seem too eager.

"Form lines!" he ordered.

Nothing happened. Slowly the boy raised his whip. He cracked it loudly. It was the signal to carry out the order.

The group suddenly broke up. The other boys cracked their whips too. There was a moment of pandemonium, as the women quickly sorted themselves out, each desperately trying to reach her proper place. There was a scream from a sulky looking girl who was slow in moving, and another from an older women who had mistaken her place. Then there was silence and stillness again. From the speed with which they had formed lines, it was clear that it was a manoeuvre they had to practice frequently.

The women now stood in three perfect lines of twenty four in each line, with a space of five yards between each line - enough for horses and riders to pass down the lines.

They were, I saw, in a perfect order of descending height, with the shortest girl on the left of the line and the tallest on the right.

I rode my horse towards the front line.

CHAPTER 15 - MADAME DE SAVOURY IS FOUND

I started to ride down the front line. It consisted of twenty four young white women. Each was looking straight ahead.

Occasionally I stopped my horse. I would reach down and stroke a girl's hair, lift another's breast or test the softness of another's cheek. Each would momentarily look up at me, dumbly pleading. I pointed to a dark haired young woman.

"You!" I said. "Step forward."

Nervously she stepped out of the line and fell to her knees in front of my horse, putting her head down to kiss his hooves.

"You have permission to speak to me," I said in Lingua Franca.

"Yes ... yes, Master," said the girl hesitantly, as if struggling to find the words. Her head was still lowered at my horse's hooves. Her long naked back was prettily curved, showing her large breasts hanging down below her.

"You have permission to kneel up ... now!" I snapped my fingers and pointed to the ground below my riding boots. I did not want the boys to think that I did not know how to treat a slave girl.

Hastily, on her knees, she scrambled round, then knelt up. She rose up off her ankles so that her face was level with my boot. She looked straight ahead. Again with one hand she held up her breast to show her number.

"How old are you?"

She hesitated. Then she spoke with difficulty in Italian, which is very similar to Lingua Franca. "Twenty four, I think, Master."

"And how long have you been here?"

Again she hesitated. "I think this will be my fifth mating season, so just over five years ... Master." She added this quickly, her eyes on my trailing whip.

"Where do you come from?"

"From Calabria, Master. I was captured by the corsairs with several other girls whilst walking along a country path on our way to a wedding. In Marsa I was bought by a farmer and then shortly afterwards my present Masters captured me and put me into their herd."

"Have you rewarded them every spring?"

"Oh yes Master, every year, and once twins," she said proudly. "And it was very difficult to run fast, carrying them, for they were both so heavy ... I thought I would die being made to run up the hills when I was so hugely swollen. But when I dropped the little twin boys one day, everyone was thrilled. The Amenoukal himself told me that I he was pleased! He even gave me a piece of cake. It was the only piece of cake I have had in five years." She sighed. "But I earned my blue stripe!"

She pointed at her left arm. Tattooed on it were five chevrons, like a sergeant's stripes. One was blue, the other four red. I saw that the other women in the herd had red chevrons tattooed on their arms. Some had many chevrons. Many had one or two blue chevrons. Some had a green one. Clearly the red chevrons recorded a single child, blue for twins and green for triplets.

"The Amenoukal has told the boys that he wants me to earn a green chevron this time. But I'm scared. Three would be so heavy for running."

"What were the twins like?"

"Very big and very black, Master, but very sweet." Her eyes began to fill with tears at the memory of the little black creatures who had been so cruelly taken from her.

"Is there any escape for you?" I asked.

"Oh no Master!" she cried, lowering her eyes to the ground. "We must not even think about escape. I am happy in the herd." I saw that several of the nearby members of the herd shrank back in alarm at the mere mention of the word.

"What of the other women?"

"We are not allowed to talk. But we have all been taught that there is no escape and that our role is to breed Haratin for the tribe. We have no choice in the matter."

"Get back into line and resume silence!" I ordered. Hastily she scuttled away to her place in the ranks. She was a credit to the boy herdsmen's discipline and training.

One of the boys rode up alongside me.

"She's a pretty little thing," he said. "She performs well. My older brother says she is one of the best. Would you like her for your manly needs? It will take only a moment to put a lead on her collar."

To be sure the slut was a lovely specimen, a fine example of these women, heavily breasted and wide hipped.

"Thank you," I said, "but I think I'll have a look at the others."

"There is a good one," said the boy. We had turned down along the second line. He was pointing at an auburn haired beauty.

I looked at the woman's right arm. Seven red chevrons were tattooed on it.

"Because of the routine to which the breeding herd is subjected," explained the boy in halting formal Arabic, after seeing my look of surprise, "they keep their beauty despite being mated every year. She is very popular with the young men of the tribe." He paused. "She is my favourite too."

These boys certainly started young, I thought. But she was not the woman I was looking for.

I rode down the line and turned down the third and last line.

Suddenly I saw her!

I saw two distinctive black beauty spots on a shapely breast. I remembered the rest of her description: a typical dark haired French woman in her late twenties, medium height, good figure, dark eyes. It all fitted! And no red chevrons tattooed on her arm, which showed that she was a new arrival. I felt my heart pounding.

It was definitely her!

I pointed to her.

"You!" cried the boy at my side. "Obeisance!"

He cracked his whip. Madame de Savoury, who I now saw was a pretty creature, and as fascinating as Achmet Abdulla had described her, crawled to the dirty front hooves of my horse and began to lick them eagerly. She had already been well trained.

"Up!" ordered the boy. He and another boy each snapped a lead onto her collar. She was now standing helplessly between the two boys' horses.

The third boy, meanwhile, had cracked his whip warningly.

"Reform!" he ordered. I saw all the women tense. He cracked his whip again and instantly the lines broke up and the women all reformed into a tightly pressed circle of naked, silent and still women.

"Back to the valley!" he ordered. At the crack of his whip the tightly packed herd ran down quickly the hill, followed by the third boy on his horse. Not until they had reached the floor of the little valley did they break up, each going off on her own, to resume grubbing in the ground for the wild turnips they so hungrily searched for, and reaching up into the bushes for berries.

The two remaining boys trotted up to me. Madame de Savoury was running between them on her bare feet, the ends of the leashes now held in the boys' hands. Politely they presented them to me. I saw that there was a snap catch on these ends too. I snapped them both onto my right stirrup. The girl was now doubly fastened to my horse. She would have to follow his every movement if she were not to be pulled off her feet and dragged by the collar round her neck.

One of the boys rode off to join his colleague on the other side of the valley. They would be watching the herd carefully. These women were under just as strict discipline as those in my harem.

The boy who was still with me pointed to some trees.

"That's where the young men of the tribe usually take them," he grinned. "You can wash her in the little stream there, and you won't be disturbed."

I turned my horse towards the trees. I urgently needed to be alone with the woman at my stirrup: we had some business to settle. She hastily moved round with the horse. I could hardly believe that I really had her chained to my stirrup.

The boy waved a cheerful goodbye. "Enjoy yourself with her. Make sure you bring her back before sundown." He pointed to the red mark between her shoulder blades. "She was mated recently, so it will be quite safe to use her."

I trotted down to the trees. She ran prettily and effortlessly. Clearly the boys had got her fit. Her breasts swung and bounced as she ran. I could feel my manhood swelling at the sight. She was indeed an attractive young woman. This would make my interrogation of her all the more interesting.

CHAPTER 16 - SPEECH IS ALLOWED

Once among the trees, I dismounted and tied my horse to a branch. The woman was still tied to the stirrup hanging from my saddle.

I loosened the girths and slipped the saddle cloth from under the saddle and spread it on the ground. Then I walked back to her.

"That rug is the same size as a Tuareg submission mat," I explained. "Whilst you are on it, you will be safe from my whip - but not from me." This was an old Tuareg custom with a captured woman. On the submission mat she had to submit, helplessly, or risk being ordered off it - in which case she would have no protection against the whip of her ravisher. "Do you understand?"

She nodded. I smiled with pleasure. I had spoken in French. It had been the second language amongst the officials of the Sublime Porte in Constantinople, so I was reasonably fluent. She had understood. She had looked at me in astonishment, hearing her native tongue spoken by what must have seemed to her to be another Moor. She did not dare say a word, however.

"You seem very quiet," I said. "Perhaps your tongue has been removed or slit as a punishment for insolence - or for talking without permission?"

She shook her head wildly and made little moaning noises that worried me for a moment. To come all this way, and then find that the woman could really no longer speak would indeed be one of fate's little ironies.

"Put out your tongue," I ordered. I felt it. It was quite normal. A feeling of relief and anticipation spread over me.

"So," I said, "we have established that if I give you permission to speak you will be capable of doing so?"

She nodded her head vigorously. It had been an impressive demonstration of the discipline under which Tuaregs kept the white beauties of their breeding herd.

"Perhaps," I mused, "I should not complicate matters by allowing you to speak."

I realised, of course, that few of the young Tuareg tribesmen who might have used her for their pleasure would have had a common language with her. No one would have bothered to teach her Tuareg or Arabic, and here in the interior Lingua Franca is little known and French even less. So I could see that this would be a unique opportunity for her.

She made piteous, begging noises.

"Is it a long time since you were allowed to speak?" I asked.

She nodded.

"Do you really want to be allowed to speak?" I asked casually, as it were a matter of little account.

She nodded desperately. I unfastened her collar leashes from the stirrup and held them in my hand. She looked at me inquiringly, her eyes huge.

"Very well then, show me how you have been taught to greet a man," I ordered harshly.

She fell to her knees. She lowered her head to my dust and mud covered boots and eagerly started to clean them with her tongue, then polish them with her breasts.

I looked down at the pretty woman, so eagerly awaiting permission to speak, to tell me the things I had come here to discover.

Holding her collar leashes taut in one hand, I pulled her up again. Then I began to run my hand down her lithe body. I felt her nipples spring to life against the palm of my hand and she gave a little moan.

"Keep silent," I warned. I saw her glance at my whip which I had held in the same hand as the leashes. I moved it slowly into my free hand. Holding her immobile by her leashes with one hand, I was ready to apply the whip with the other. With a shudder, she tried to back away, her breath coming in little gasps.

"Keep still!" I ordered. "Remember that when you are allowed onto the submission mat, then you will be safe from my whip. But you will only be allowed onto it if you show full submission first."

She nodded vigorously again, her eyes fixed on my whip in genuine fear.

I felt that it was time to start her serious arousal. An aroused woman speaks more freely in her acute desire for immediate relief. I slid one of the leashes to the back of her collar. I let go of the end which I had been holding and used it to tie her wrists together, high behind her back. She would not be able to interfere as I played with her body. 'A tied woman, is already a half aroused woman,' is an old Turkish saying, and a very true one.

In my harem I had found that three strokes, slowly and deliberately given, firmly but not too hard, and with each stroke begged for and counted aloud by the girl, rarely fails to arouse a woman. It is something that is inherent in a woman's psyche - or anyway in a white woman's.

That women were well aware of this was borne out, I had noticed, by the way they behaved if allowed to play with each other. Invariably the dominant one would use her hands or a slipper to smack her more submissive partner, and thus quickly bring her into enjoying her role. Again, this pattern of behaviour was something that I had observed and experimented with in my harem. Women make fascinating toys to play with!

"Are you familiar with the use of the whip?" I asked innocently.

Once again the pretty woman nodded wildly. No woman would have been herded by those young boys and not have a very thorough understanding of the power of the whip.

"I am going to release you from silence, slave. But I warn you, I shall thrash you if you speak one word without permission, except in replying to a question from me. Tell me that you understand."

"I ... understand," she said slowly as if she found speaking difficult. She had an entrancingly husky voice. I was delighted that she spoke in French. She must indeed be the woman I sought. Even if she were not, I told myself consolingly, it would still be delightful to enjoy her.

I raised my whip threateningly. "Have you not forgotten a certain word?" I said angrily.

"I understand ... Master," she said hastily.

I nodded approvingly. With a woman, as with a horse, it is important to establish the desired relationship right from the outset.

"Remember," I said, "on the submission mat you will be safe from the whip." She turned as if to run to it. But I still held one of her leashes in my hand. She was brought up short, like a dog on a lead.

"No not yet," I laughed. "First you are going to have three strokes from my whip, to make you realise that I am in charge. Then you will perform for me on the mat. If your performance is not satisfactory, then you will be led off the mat and whipped. Now tell your Master, you understand."

"I ... understand, Master."

"Good ... Now bend over!"

With her hands fastened behind her back to her collar, she made a delightful picture of female helplessness as she bent forward. I pushed her neck down, and to prevent herself from falling she had to bend her knees and separate her legs. I was amused to see her hands desperately trying to reach down to protect her soft buttocks, but I had deliberately bound them too high for that.

"Before each stroke you will in your own carefully chosen words, beg for it. If I feel that you have not begged sufficiently humbly and eagerly, then you will still receive the stroke, but it will not count towards the three. Nor will it count if you fall to the ground."

I saw her give a little wriggle, Was it imagination, or did I already see something glistening and moist upon her body lips?

"Now think carefully and then beg."

There was a pause, then the words came out slowly, shyly and with difficulty.

"Master ... this ... slave begs her Master ... to be so kind ... as to give her ... the first stroke. But, please, not too hard."

"Good, that's very good," I patted her on the buttocks encouragingly. "But don't you dare try to tell me your Master how hard to beat you. That is for him to decide. You are just a slave - you do what he says. So, I'm afraid, the first stroke will not count."

She gave a sob. I waited. I could see her heavy breasts rising and falling in her agitation as they hung beneath her. Her breath came in little gasps. Doubtless, she would be anticipating the pain. Then suddenly I brought the whip down across her buttocks.

A scream echoed round the grove. I saw her bound hands desperately trying to reach down to where a little red weal was spreading across her buttocks.

"Now you will kiss the whip and thank it prettily and passionately."

She did so. In all she had five strokes.

"Now crawl to the submission mat."

Swiftly she did so, grateful to be within its temporary safety.

"On your back," I ordered. "Hands to your side, palms up, right knee raised."

Wincing from the pain of the beating, she complied. I felt that I had now completely asserted my authority over her.

I knelt down beside her and began to examine the creature in my power. It was just as I had expected. The beating had thoroughly aroused her.

"Oh! ... Oh!"

Her dark eyes were huge. The tell tale marks of her arousal began to appear on her neck. Her eyes now had a glazed look and were fixed on me, wonderingly, adoringly.

It was time to take my hands away.

She cried out in French. "No! No! Your hands! Your hands, don't take your hands away, please Master."

"Were you given permission to speak?"

She looked terrified. "No, Master, I'm sorry," she cried out. "I beg for mercy."

I put my hand on her beauty bud. She began to pant. I felt her tight muscles relax. It was soon time to take my hands away.

I had to be careful not to disclose my particular interest in her. I had to pretend that to me she was just another slave.

I lay down alongside the still kneeling woman. I let her kiss me. I let her crawl into my arms. One hand was still on her beauty bud. I saw an astonished and delighted expression light up her face.

"I wonder how such a pretty little slave came to be in the breeding herd of the Teghe-Mellet?" I asked kindly.

"You are the first man to bother to ask me that. The first man here to even speak to me kindly. The first to allow me to speak. The first man to consider my own desires as a woman and not treat me purely as an animal. The others would just take me from behind then throw me aside without a word."

I smiled. She was falling into my trap. Of course, for the randy young men of the tribe she was just a dumb animal whose needs could be ignored. She was just a new two legged brood mare, anxious to please to avoid the whip, but dumb.

"Are you pleased to be allowed to speak, then?" I asked gently.

"Oh, yes, Master," the woman said fervently. She still spoke slowly and with difficulty - thereby making it all the easier for me to understand her. "It is strange and wonderful to be able to speak again, after all this time."

"But do the women never speak together?" I asked.

"Just occasionally, the odd whispered word in Lingua Franca. But never a conversation, not even a sentence. Those awful young boys are too strict and watchful. We are not even allowed to sing to ourselves. We are never left alone. And the punishment for trying to talk is six strokes of the boy's whip. It's inhuman."

She stopped, wondering if she had said too much.

"Go on," I said encouragingly. I wanted her to pour out her thoughts.

"It's terrible, not being allowed to speak. I just don't know why we are kept like animals in this herd. What's it all for anyway? You simply won't believe this ... several of us are taken by Negroes each evening. Even I was." She shivered at the recollection. "But why? I can't ask any of the other women."

She paused. I was fascinated to learn that she did not yet know that she was in a Haratin breeding herd. I looked down at her flat belly. There were no signs of any stretch marks. Her forthcoming child would evidently be her first. I looked at the swell of her hips. She would, I thought, make do excellently for the tribe. They would not sell her cheaply. I wondered what she would look like soon with a swollen belly and how it would effect her ability to run.

"But soon the French will come and free all us wretched Christian slave women!" she cried triumphantly.

Suddenly, my heart was in my mouth as I heard these words. But I controlled my longing to follow them up.

"Wretched Christian slave women?" I repeated. "Surely you are lucky to be in the hands of Masters who care for you?"

"Care for us!" she cried scornfully. I was succeeding in getting her angry. Soon she would no longer mind what she said. "You can't imagine how utterly degrading it is for a cultured European woman to be a slave in Barbary. My first Master was a rich old man, a pervert, who bought well educated, delicate white women to amuse him, not in his harem, but toiling under the hot sun in the quarries on his estate whilst he watched in the shade."

"So how did you end up here?" I asked, knowing the answer of course, but wanting to seem sympathetic. At the same time I touched her again momentarily. "Go on!"

"Oh!" she cried. She was now learning that she would get pleasure if she answered my questions. It was like training an animal!

"One night the estate was raided by this tribe of Tuaregs, and here I am. It is even worse than being used as a labourer on my former Master's estate."

She looked up at me gratefully. "You are the first man here to treat me as a woman," she repeated. "Who are you? Where did you learn French?"

It was time to be severe again. I raised my whip warningly. At the same time I reached down to touch her again. She moaned.

"I am the one who asks the questions." I said. "Who are you, and how did you come to be a white slave in Barbary? Tell me!"

"I am the wife of a French Colonel on the Staff of Marshal Murat."

I felt the hairs on my neck rise. I tried to hide my excitement. Could she give us the details of the French plans? I tried to provoke her again.

"A likely story!" I said scornfully. "You're just a French peasant girl."

"I'm not, I'm not - you'll see who I am when the French troops land and release us all. Soon!"

"Bah!" I said. "What would a mere woman know about that?"

"I know all about it!" she said proudly. "My husband was planning the invasion, which will be commanded by Marshal

Murat. That's why Napoleon has sent Murat to replace the Emperor's brother, Joseph, as king of Naples, whilst Joseph goes off to be King of Spain. Murat and my husband have the task of capturing Sicily, and then invading North Africa."

"But even if they did land," I said with a false show of disbelief, "the tribesmen will throw them back into the sea."

"Not if they are welcomed, when they land, by the Emir of Rebar with a hundred thousand armed men."

I tried not to show my alarm. The Emir of Rebar was the Turks' main ally amongst the inland tribal leaders. If he was secretly in touch with the French, then the situation could be very serious indeed. But it was important not to arouse the woman's suspicions - or she would clam up completely.

"What rubbish," I laughed, "the Emir of Rebar is a firm friend of the Turks. And anyway the English Navy will never let you get here."

"Well, they let us get all the way to Egypt from Toulon in '98 and that was much further than the short journey from Syracuse in Sicily to the Tunisian coast. Anyway the English fleet will be decoyed away by a false expedition that will be mounted in Bari and which they will think is aimed at the Dardanelles - so they'll be well out of the way!"

A deception plan! My mind was reeling. A deception plan to make the English think that the French were aiming at the Dardanelles - the gateway to Constantinople itself. That would certainly keep the Royal Navy away from the Tunisian coast for long enough for a powerful expeditionary force to be landed.

But the Pasha would need some convincing of the perfidy of his main ally. He would want to hear from the woman's own mouth and in greater detail. He would want her in his torture chamber to be sure that he had emptied her of all possible information. And, if the British were to believe our story, we would need to know just where and when the landing would take place - and in what strength.

It would be best, I decided, if I pretended that I was so impressed by this woman's performance that I wanted to buy her. I would offer a price that would make it worth their while, whilst not so high as to arouse their suspicions. They were used to a pregnant woman fetching a higher price, and I must go along with that.

88

Meanwhile I must, of course, enjoy her services now. I suspected that the boy herdsmen were probably watching. Clearly I must put her through the full gamut. She was an attractive and sensuous woman. It was a duty that I would enjoy.

CHAPTER 17 - MADAME DE SAVOURY CHANGES MASTER

It was towards evening when I broached the subject with Attici. We were returning from watching the evening matings of the tribe's largest Negroes with those of the girls who were judged to be ready.

"I trust you enjoyed the woman you took this afternoon?" he had asked.

"Indeed, brother," I replied. I appeared to ponder. "I think that my Master, the Pasha, would deeply appreciate the gift of her as a slave for his private galliot. She has just the figure that he likes to use for pulling an oar. You would make him a friend, and every day he would see her and be reminded of you."

"Give that one to the Pasha!" said Attici in genuine dismay. "But she is most valuable - and pregnant these last few weeks."

"I do know that the Pasha is being much disturbed by complaints of the raids of the Tuareg, especially of the Teghe-Mellet," I murmured. "He is under strong pressure to use the Janissaries to teach them a lesson."

"Is he indeed?" said Attici, blanching.

"But he has always said that searching for Teghe-Mellet would be like looking for a particular grain of sand in the desert. I think I can persuade him to leave you in peace - particularly if he feels he can rely on you should the Christians ever try to invade."

"We will do anything to keep the Christians out," replied Attici. "He only has to send word, and we will raise a thousand armed men from amongst the neighbouring tribes, and ten thousand from the rest of the Tuareg ... But that woman! The Pasha does not intend to ruin us, surely?"

"It would be very much in your interest for him to think that you have sent him such a woman as a sign of your friendship. But secretly I will give you more than her worth in gold, so that you can replace her in the slave markets, or mount a new raid on the long suffering farmers."

Attici laughed aloud.

"You are a clever man - and my friend as well as that of the Pasha. You will find her in a basket hanging on the side of one of your camels tomorrow morning! Meanwhile we shall celebrate tonight with two other Christian girls. Come, my friend, come!"

I did not feel that the Pasha would mind if I were to enjoy myself tonight even though I was on duty. I had obtained what he wanted, quickly and cheaply.

Attici led the way to a tent that was set apart from the others. A large Negro was standing on guard outside it. From inside it came young girlish laughter and young European voices.

I felt a sudden pang - I thought for a moment that one of the voices sounded just like that of Henrietta Hamilton. But, of course, it wasn't. She was back in Marsa, incarcerated in the harem of the Pasha. Out here I had almost succeeded in putting her out of my mind, but back in Marsa, seeing the Pasha every day, I should be thinking of her constantly.

Oh if only the Pasha had not taken me to the slave dealers, I thought. Then I would never have seen her, or even known about her.

"Come," called Attici. "Let us amuse ourselves!"

I followed him into the tent ...

CHAPTER 18 - THE PASHA DECIDES

"Listen!" said the Pasha.

Through the open door that led down into the dungeon, I heard the crack of the Negro's black corbash. There was a swishing noise and the dull thud as it landed across the woman's backside, then a terrible scream.

The Pasha gestured to the door. A pretty white eunuch page boy quickly closed it, shutting out the noise and the screams.

"She has confirmed all that you told me," said the Pasha.

I had brought the basket containing Madame de Savoury to the Pasha's palace the previous evening. It had taken nearly a week to return to Marsa from the encampment of the Teghe-Mellet.

Every evening, after we had pitched our camp and eaten, Zachet had brought her to my tent, chained and naked, and fastened her to the tent pole. Every night I had used her, not allowing her speech. I did not want her to start asking where she was being taken or why. I wanted to deliver her to the Pasha, unsuspecting the importance of her story about the French plans for the invasion of North Africa. I did not want her to start making up another story to disguise the truth.

Each morning Zachet, the Pasha's Berber page boy, had put Madame de Savoury back into her small basket which was strapped to the side of a camel. I did not want to risk her being seen by any marauding Tuaregs we might run into. To lose her at this stage, after all my efforts at finding her, would have been disastrous.

The Pasha was delighted when I had suddenly arrived with her, and immediately ordered that she be sent down to his dungeons. But when I told him what she had said to me about the treachery of the Emir of Rebar, and of the deception plans to make the British fleet think that the expedition was aimed at the Dardanelles rather than the Barbary States, then his face had gone grim.

"I shall interrogate her tomorrow," was his comment, "and get the full story out of her. But you, my son, must now get back to the joys of your harem. You have served the Sultan very well, you deserve a little pleasure and relaxation."

I acknowledged his compliment with a bow. I did not like to tell him that I had enjoyed Madame de Savoury every night for the past week.

"Come back here tomorrow evening," were his final words, "and we will finalise plans."

I had found young Abdul in charge of my harem: Matrak, of course, would be running the training camp. The Pasha and Matrak must have continued to buy girls discreetly in small numbers, to keep the market prices low and avoid any speculation as to why such a large number of European women were being bought by them.

My girls had all been thrilled to see me back. None of them, of course, had any relief whilst I was away. I had been nervous lest they might have been unfaithful by seeking self gratification in the absence of Matrak. But Abdul proudly told me that he caught two of them trying to play with themselves.

Etta, the newest slave, had been caught trying to give herself relief under the bedclothes. Francesca, more cunningly as befitted the oldest of my slave girls, had been caught in the seclusion of the harem garden. In both cases, their forbidden activities had been given away by the ringing of the little bells on their special bracelets before any harm had been done. Abdul had thrashed them in front of the other girls as a warning against infidelity, as he termed it - a joke in itself for, of course, none of them would have had so much as a glimpse of another man in my absence. But the Moslem concept of infidelity in a harem is much stricter than the Christian one.

Young Abdul was convinced that no other girls had tried, and that he had succeeded in keeping all of them virtuous and faithful during my absence. No wonder they had been so excited at my sudden return! I could see that Abdul would go far as a black eunuch when he grew up. He was still only a boy and yet clearly my women were frightened of him.

Abdul made each of the women, in turn, pass in front of a screen behind which I was sitting. They were dressed in their erotic formal harem dress, or perhaps I should say undress, and each was trying to look as beautiful and appealing as possible.

As Abdul called the name of each woman, she walked in front of the screen, pivoted round prettily and then fall silently to her hands and knees in humble obeisance with her forehead touching the floor, her arms outstretched towards me and her long hair flung forward. Then raising her head slightly, and looking up submissively at the screen, each was allowed to lisp her love and adoration for her Master and to beg him to choose her for his pleasure. She was also allowed to say why she felt he could get more pleasure from her than from any of the other girls.

There is no doubt that controlling the sensuousness of a group of passionate women, and keeping them frustrated, is a most satisfying part of slave ownership.

I had much enjoyed watching as Abdul called the name of the next woman, and the girl kneeling in front of my screen would rise and humbly withdraw backwards, her hands clasped over her breasts and her head lowered in a gesture of respect.

It was a charming sight. I found it difficult to choose which woman I wanted for my bed. Each was so attractive in a different way. Each was clearly desperately hoping that she would be chosen. However, my journey deep into Tuareg territory had highlighted for me the attraction of the slenderness and fine features of Berber women. Moreover thanks to Madame de Savoury I had recently almost satiated myself with the delights of a European woman.

"Muneerah and Lala," I called out to Abdul - much to the chagrin of my European slaves.

It had been a night of intense pleasure as the two young girls rivalled each other in a display of uninhibited sensuousness that a Christian girl would have been embarrassed to display to a man, even after explicit lessons from Matrak and his cane ...

But back to the present ...

"I do not think we shall get any more out of her," the Pasha said. "She has already confirmed all that she told you about the Emir of Rebar and the false plan to invade the Dardanelles. She has also given us details of just where the landing near Tunis will be made and how many troops will be involved. I am sure that I already know all that she knows ..."

"What will you do with her?" I asked.

"Like her former maid, she must be kept in isolation. No word of what she knows must leak out - anyway not until the French threat is over and the Emir of Rebar has again become a loyal servant of the Sultan."

"So I suppose ..." I started to say.

"Yes, she will join her maid, pulling an oar in my galley," laughed the Pasha.

I tried to imagine the rather haughty Madame de Savoury chained naked to her oar. It would, I suppose, not be too awful after her stint as a quarry slave of Achmet Abdulla and then in the girl herd of the Teghe-Mellet.

"Perhaps," the Pasha mused, "when all this has died down, I will put her and her maid into my harem. They would make an amusing pair. But all that can wait." The Pasha's voice suddenly acquired a decisive tone and he patted my knee in an affectionate way. "You have done magnificently, my son. Now comes the equally difficult bit - deciding what should be done to take advantage of the information she has given us."

The Pasha got down to business remarkably quickly for an oriental. It was interesting to see the quick Turkish decisiveness that had once made the Ottoman Empire the fear of all Europe.

"Later," he said, "with the Blessing of Allah, you must go off to Malta to tell the British authorities all that we know. With the British so suspicious of Turkish intentions, they will be more impressed by you, a former British officer, than anyone else - even if you are a renegade."

I flushed momentarily with anger, but I knew it was true. The British would listen to me far more readily than they would a Turk.

"But even more urgently, I want you to leave shortly with your coffles of European slave women, and deal with the Emir of Rebar - and any other waverers amongst the tribal leaders inland."

"But will the offer of a few white girls for his harem really be enough to detach him from the French?" I said.

The Pasha gave a cunning look. He reached into his rich and voluminous robes and pulled out a letter in Arabic script.

"This," he said mysteriously, "is the key to recapturing the loyalties of the Emir of Rebar!"

The Pasha handed the letter to me.

"For generations," he explained, for he knew that I still read Arabic slowly, "much of the wealth of the Emirs of Rebar has come from their highly successful blond slave breeding farm high up in the cool and healthy climate of the mountains. His breeding lines are said to go back to the wives of certain Spanish grandees captured when Tunis was recaptured from Spain in what the Christians call their sixteenth century. He crossed these with some Swedish and North German mercenaries who were captured at the same time and who are also, of course, blond and blue eyed. The result has until recently been a highly successful operation."

"Yes, I see," I said. I had heard of such special slave breeding farms.

"The fool of an Emir thinks that the French will simply occupy the Barbary Ports and their coastline and not bother about the interior," continued the Pasha. "He does not seem to realise that a successful French invasion would inevitably force him to close down his extremely profitable white slave breeding farm. But in this letter he says that his best breeding lines have suddenly been wrecked by an outbreak of disease in his farm. Apparently it has killed many of his stock. He now has the effrontery to ask for my assistance in replacing them - little dreaming that I know of his treachery."

The Pasha looked me in the face.

"So you can see what your highest priority should be now," he said.

"You mean I should ..." I stammered hesitantly.

"I mean that you should arrive in his territory with some truly fabulous blond men and women. You should show them to him. You should tell him that they are intended to be a present for him from me, to help him get him going again, but only in return for certain guarantees - and perhaps in return, in due course, for a gift to me of two of his favourite daughters for my harem. They will be a sign of our undying friendship - and of a way of ensuring his loyalty, for I swear I would behead those daughters if I have any more trouble from him. You will then tell him of the French plans to take over the whole country, and how they will immediately free all white slaves and ban all slave breeding, which would kill the golden egg for him. I think he will immediately swing round again and renew his allegiance to the Sultan, the Commander of the Believers, may Allah send him a thousand blessings ... Now let us get down to details."

CHAPTER 19 - PURCHASES

"But is she responsive?" I asked the burly Negro whipmaster.

He grinned and pulled the pretty girl up by her hair into a kneeling position. Then with his left hand, gripping both her hair and her wrist manacles, he pulled her head right back. Her naked body was now arched backwards and well displayed. She could not see down. Keeping her in that position, he put his right hand down onto her belly. The contrast between his jet black hand and the whiteness of her belly was very noticeable.

Slowly he began to move his right hand.

Nothing happened at first.

Then suddenly she screamed. "No! No!"

The Negro took his time. He was an expert in white European women. Soon she was sobbing.

"No! Oh! Yes! Yes! ... No don't stop!"

He released her and flung her down on the block. She was crimson with embarrassment and sobbing with shame ...

It was a week now since I had delivered young Madame de Savoury to the tender mercies of the Pasha and his Negro guards.

It was also a week since the Pasha had given me back the original bag of gold, less what he used to pay for the girls that I bought before leaving for the interior, and less what he and Matrak had paid for the girls they bought for me. I was now to use the remaining gold to complete the purchases.

Matrak had come back from the training camp to advise me how many women we still needed to buy, and of what type and stamp.

He told me that he had already had a dozen of the most beautiful girls covered by the Pasha's Dinka guards. They would form my principal display team, running, with their swelling bellies exposed, either chained to my stirrup and carrying an umbrella over my head, or chained to the back of my saddle side by side in two lines, one behind the other. They would make an eye-catching display team, guaranteed to arouse the cruel sensuality of the tribal rulers.

Half a dozen tall girls would be required to give to the Emir of Tatra for his coffee enterprise, and another two dozen for bribing other Emirs and Shareefs. I would keep the display girls back to the last. The girls to be given away should be in matched pairs, as identical as possible in shape and size, so as to have a greater effect on the recipients. They might have bought the occasional European girl before, but they would never, I was sure, have been given a matched pair.

Similarly, it was important that the girls in each of the two lines of the display team should be as identical as possible to give the greatest effect.

There was also the difficult problem of finding suitable blond women for the Emir of Rebar. Such women were rare in the Mediterranean and rarely came onto the market. When they did, they tended to be fiendishly expensive - as I had seen for myself when the Pasha had bought the lovely blond Henrietta for a price

96

that I could not even have begun to pay. Matrak, however, seemed quite relaxed about this problem. Perhaps he knew something that I did not.

Anyway, apart from the blond women for the Emir of Rebar, it looked as though we would need about forty girls, including the display team. The remainder would form two coffles of about fifteen each. The precious recruits for the Emir of Rebar's breeding farm would, of course, be on a separate coffle.

I found on my return that we now had nearly thirty women. These included four lead girls, two for the display team and one for each of the main coffles. These lead girls were trained pleasure slaves already well broken into their slavery. Matrak had bought two from the display platform of a dealer in the Tal Basr slave market who specialised in second hand pleasure slaves. They bore the brand of a high class pleasure house in Marsa, having been sold by their previous owner to make way for fresh newly captured girls. Matrak had contacted the chief black eunuch under whose control they had worked, and he had confirmed that they were all well trained submissive creatures who were eager to please and who had no vices.

The role of these slaves would be comparable to that of prefects in a school, whilst the Negro cofflemasters would be more like strict school masters, with Matrak as head master.

Finding two lead girls already pregnant for the display team had been more difficult. Matrak had felt that it was important for each line to have one more experienced slave as its leader. He had found what he was looking for in the booth of another specialist slave dealer.

These two line leaders bore the brand of a well known Rais, or corsair captain. Knowing him as I did, I was sure that they would have been well disciplined and would prove to be good lead girls for the display team, setting a good example as they pranced along behind my trotting horse. Matrak had contacted the Rais' chief black eunuch and had found that there was a quite normal reason for the Rais selling them. He just liked to have a rapid turnover of the girls in his harem.

The first decision I had made on my return was to place an order for five well matched pairs of girls from the waterfront establishment of Abu Hussein, the owner of the caique which I had inspected earlier on.

He had just bought wholesale, as part of a job lot, all the young females captured in a raid on a certain Calabrian village. These girls were now being processed in his slave pens. Because of in-breeding, these isolated Calabrian villages often produced girls of a distinctive stamp with similar features and of a similar build. Moreover, they often had a look that was a clear throwback to the Greeks who had colonised Calabria before the days of the Roman Empire.

Abu Hussein had assured me, therefore, that he would have no difficulty in meeting my requirement for pairs of identical height, looks and conformation.

I prefer to buy girls from a leading professional dealer with a reputation to preserve. Not only do you know what you are buying, but also he will always take back a girl who proves unsuitable, and offer another in her place.

Now Matrak and I had come to the rival establishment of Abu Said, the dealer whose pit I had inspected two months previously, to make some of our final purchases. This was why his Negro whipmaster was testing this girl for response.

"You see, Master," he said with a grin as he wiped his hand on his robe, "she feel plenty. She plenty wet."

Matrak put his hand down too. He liked to check things for himself which was why I liked to bring him along when choosing a girl. He nodded, satisfied with what he had found.

But I knew it was not only her passionate responsiveness that Matrak wanted to see tested. All the girls I was buying also needed good strong legs to stand up to the march which lay ahead of them and a good strong back so that they could each carry a good load as a pack animal on the march.

An Arab found little pleasure in controlling, and keeping frustrated, a cold white woman. That was why Matrak and I had been watching with interest the passionate writhings of the girl on the block as she had been tested by the Negro.

But we were also looking for a cheerful, happy disposition. This would be a great help on the march as the chained girls realised the appalling fate that lay ahead of them.

There was a dozen blocks, in two rows, down one side of the hall. Down the other side were pens for sheep and goats, stalls for donkeys and large comfortable straw lined boxes for the numerous beautiful Arab horses in which Abu Said also dealt.

In the center of each block a large ring had been cemented into the stone. Each girl was attached to this ring by a chain some four feet long. This ended in an iron collar which locked round her neck. Each girl, of course, still wore the wrist manacles that I had seen on the girls in the animal pits.

"Run her," I told the Negro.

She was led over to a sandy arena where an Arab groom stood holding a lunging rein in one hand and a long whip in the other. He soon had her prancing round the little arena whilst Matrak and I watched her carefully. There was no sign of lameness and she moved very nicely and evenly. I looked inquiringly at Matrak, and he nodded.

"I'll take her," I said. "Put her with the others."

The Negro wrapped a shawl around the naked girl. She grabbed it eagerly with her chained wrists, delighted at last to be able to cover her nakedness in front of so many immaculately dressed men. Indeed, the contrast between a slave girl's nakedness on the block, a nakedness accentuated by her freshly shaven body lips, and the beautiful long robes, burnouses, cloaks with gold thread and edgings, huge brightly coloured turbans, and Arab kuffayah head-dresses encircled with gold encrusted aighals, worn by the grave faced men examining her, always acutely embarrassed white women exposed for sale.

As the Negro led her away, I noticed another girl being led from the preparation room on a chain. Her hair had been well brushed. Her eyes and face had been carefully painted. Her body had been powdered to accentuate the whiteness of her skin. Her freshly shorn body lips had been beautifully painted scarlet, and outlined in black, as had her nipples and her mouth. She was fastened to the block vacated by the girl I had just bought.

That was Abu Said's technique when business was brisk: never have too many girls on display, but as each is sold bring out another in her place.

The blocks were placed sufficiently apart from each other to enable buyers to examine each girl at their leisure. A Negro whipmaster was in charge of each line of six blocks, and if he saw that a prospective buyer was looking interested in a girl, he could come and put her through her paces - making her assume in succession the various display positions she had been taught in the preparation room.

The whipmasters received commission on each sale. They would be very angry if a girl did not display herself well. The girls were constantly being encouraged to show themselves off by sharp little taps of the Negro's whip. Despite being desperately shy and ashamed of their nakedness, their natural fear of the Negro's whip soon ensured that they displayed themselves in a proper manner.

If several buyers were interested in a girl, then the Negro had the authority to conduct an immediate auction, as he put the girl through her display.

These Negroes are experts at describing the good features of a girl and the future delights she could be forced to give a strong master.

"Put your fingers in her mouth, Effendi. Look at her white teeth. Let her suck your finger. Imagine pleasure she give you."

"Let her lick palm of your hand, Effendi. Imagine tongue licking you beneath bed clothes."

"Feel soft breast, Effendi. You think how nice when giving you milk."

"Tickle, Effendi, tickle this little bud. See how she wriggles. Imagine her wriggling under you."

A buyer could always make an offer for a girl to her Negro whipmaster. He would then paint a blue Arabic sign on her back to show that she was under offer. This often had the effect of making someone else quickly agree to pay the asking price for fear of losing her.

If business was sluggish, then to give the appearance of a brisk trade in girls and to encourage the buyers to make a purchase quickly for fear of losing a girl to someone else, the Negro would often lead an unsold girl away from the block just as if she had been sold. She would then be replaced by another similar looking girl, so that a prospective buyer would feel that this time he had better move quickly to secure the girl. Then, later, the original girl, her face and eyes made up differently, and her beauty lips, nipples and mouth painted a different colour, would appear on a different block, as if for the first time.

Abu Said and his team of black whipmasters were indeed a clever lot!

All these arrangements went back to the days when the majority of the women on display were black or local Berber girls. It came as a severe shock to the large number of European girls now being handled by Abu Said to be prepared and supervised by Negroes and to be inspected in this utterly degrading way by Arabs.

Consideration of a slave girl's anatomy does not only take place when a girl is being bought for the harem of a rich man. Even a farmer in Marsa, when buying a sturdy white girl to pull a plough alongside his asses, will also be thinking of the pleasure he will be taking from her, tethered in her stall, at the end of a long day.

Similarly, the owner of a carpet factory or mill, will when purchasing a girl be thinking of the pleasure she will give to his Negro overseers. These overseers are the key to his business achieving a high level of production. Moorish mill owners learned that there was nothing so effective for stimulating production as giving the overseers a free rein with the white girls working under them - both with their whips to punish real and imaginary laziness or carelessness, and with their rampant manhoods.

As I looked across the hall to the girl now being chained down onto the empty block, I saw that she was surprisingly self composed. Despite her nudity, and despite being chained and collared, with her beauty lips, nipples and mouth all painted a matching shade of red, she still managed to carry off an impression of superiority and insolent pride. She looked at the men clustering round her as if they were mere underlings and of no account. I did not think that it was an attitude that would be tolerated for long by the slavemasters of Marsa.

Then I saw that her belly was slightly swollen.

As she knelt forward, whilst the Negro linked her collar chain to the ring under her belly, I saw a distinguished looking Arab reach forward with both hands to part her beauty lips. I saw her try to push his hands away. Then she scuttled round to the far side of her little platform. She was certainly a striking looking young woman.

"No! Don't touch me!" she screamed. "Don't touch me."

Instantly the Negro whipmaster, unhitching his whip from his wide belt, was upon her. The men around her stepped back, looking on with interest as she now lay on her belly twisting and wriggling under the whip. It was a fairly harmless whip, for Abu Said did not want any of the delicate creatures being displayed to be seriously harmed. He relied more on fear than actual pain.

Soon the Negro stepped back. He folded the thongs of his whip under their clip and re-attached the handle to his belt. Then he posed her prettily on her block. This time when the same Arab reached forward again, parting the delicate lips with the thumb and forefinger of each hand, she did not resist.

She did however, give a little whimper as another Arab, standing at her side, bent down and carefully weighed one breast in his hand and rolled her nipples between his fingers. On the other side another Arab was weighing her gently swollen belly, and then running his hands over her hips as if judging her eventual ability to deliver her growing progeny.

But she kept quite still, with her head raised and her eyes fixed ahead, she had learned that she was now just an animal whom men might examine and caress as they pleased.

But she had shown considerable courage. This was another quality that would be needed on the march inland. She would, I thought, make a fine stirrup display girl, and in another month her belly would be showing well. I even felt my loins moving at the thought.

I would have to move quickly, for several of the Arabs were clearly very interested in acquiring her. There was not even time to consult with Matrak.

I strode towards her. I picked up the little display card.

"Beatriz, age 23. The wife of a Portuguese sea captain and pregnant by him."

Portuguese! I thought. That was quite unusual in Marsa. Clearly her husband's ship had been captured whilst on its way to a central Mediterranean port. The Portuguese were a hardy race.

"I will take her," I said, lifting up her left breast to see her asking price more clearly. "Put her with the others."

102

There were murmurs of protest from the other men round her, but I saw that the Negro was hastening to carry out my order. I had pressed a coin into his hand.

I saw Matrak looking at me curiously. He did not miss much, I thought. He would have realised that I was not merely interested in the girl as a stirrup girl. I could not help wishing that I could use the Pasha's money to buy her for my own harem!

As my beautiful purchase was led away, clutching the shawl which now hid her nakedness, she turned and looked over her shoulder at me, the man who had bought her, her eyes wide. It almost seemed as if she could not bear to take her eyes off me, despite her whipmaster's urgings to run out of the display room and into the adjoining dispatching room. She gave me a little frightened smile. I recognised it as the nervous smile that a subjugated woman instinctively gives to her master. Then just as she disappeared out of sight behind the door, she gave me a definite little wink. The little minx!

I felt a discreet touch on the hanging sleeve of my robe. It was the secretary of Abu Said. Like many such men in Marsa he was a Jew.

Officially Jews are members of a race that was despised here almost as much as Christians were. They were forced to wear a distinctive tasselled cap. They had to walk barefoot through the filth in the streets. They had to salt the heads of prisoners who had been beheaded before they were exhibited above the gates of the city. But despite all this, their cleverness and discretion made them eagerly sought out by leading merchants for positions of trust.

The Jew said nothing, but a flicker of his dark eyes beckoned Matrak and I to follow him. He led the way across the hall, through a small and unobtrusive door, and up a small staircase.

CHAPTER 20 - SWEDISH BLONDS

The gross but smiling figure of Abu Said stood waiting for us in his private room. On one side was a lattice-work screen through which he could look down onto the display hall. I saw that he would be able to watch everything that was going on. On the other side was a similar screen that looked down onto the preparation room. Two young white eunuch page boys stood against the wall, doubtlessly ready to run with his orders to the Negro in charge of the preparation room to get another girl ready or to send another into the display hall.

I could see that Abu Said ran his sales like a military operation, deploying some women, and keeping others back in reserve. The page boys drew curtains across both the lattice-work screens. Presumably Abu Said did not want us being distracted by what was going on down below. He must have something serious to discuss.

Matrak was smiling knowingly.

"I admire your choice of girls," said Abu Said with a laugh, "though that Portuguese girl you've bought may turn out to be more of a handful than you have bargained for."

"We'll have to see," I said. He had not brought me up to his room merely to discuss the disciplining of a slave girl.

He turned and clapped his hands. A huge Negro whipmaster came into the room and bowed deeply to Abu Said.

"Look at these," said the slave dealer.

The Negro pulled back a curtain in the corner of the room. There, blinking in the sudden light, and standing on a little platform, were three outstandingly attractive women.

As usual their wrists were chained, but in addition they were held upright by short chains that linked the ring at the back of their iron collars to rings set in the wall. Their wrist chains were also fastened behind their necks to the same ring. They were thus well displayed.

They looked terrified. They could not take their eyes off the Negro's whip. They did not dare to speak.

Their nudity was heightened by a leather belt fastened over their bellies from which hung identical embroidered flaps which hid their intimacies. These flaps, copied from those commonly worn by Negresses, were known in Marsa as Modesty Flaps. Slave girls much appreciated being allowed to wear one in the presence of men.

I saw that one of the women was in her thirties, whilst the other two were still in their teens. There was a definite similarity in their strikingly good looks, and this was not merely due to the fact that all three had their hair arranged, and their faces made up, identically.

What caught my attention above all was their beautiful long blond golden hair and their startlingly blue eyes. Abu Said saw my look of astonishment. Such striking blond women were rare in the Marsa slave markets, to have three on display was unheard of.

"Yes," he said, "I thought you'd be surprised. They are a mother and her two daughters. The wife and daughters of the captain of a Swedish merchant ship captured off the coast of Spain, and brought to me to sell as a special offer to one of my more discerning clients."

They were indeed a rare capture.

"Half of Marsa's elite would give a fortune to have them in their harems - if they knew of their existence. But I thought first of my loyalty to the Pasha."

I started at the mention of the Pasha. Then I laughed silently. If Abu Said knew that I was buying women on behalf of the rich old Pasha, then he must know of the bag of gold that the Pasha had given me - otherwise he would not be bothering with me.

"Moreover," he went on, "quite apart from their value as harem slaves, a reputable blond slave breeder with a reputation to keep up as regards the standard of his merchandise, would do anything to own such a group. They would enable him to start a completely new breeding line with three closely related women to put to one proven blond male. What a wonderful team to have in one's breeding pens."

I had been busy doing mental arithmetic as he spoke. Quite understandably, he would be looking for at least double the normal price for a blond woman for each of this unique group.

The slave dealer looked me in the eye. Then he suddenly spoke in Turkish, which is little understood in Marsa.

"Give them to the Emir of Rebar, and he will be so delighted that he will feed out of your hand."

I looked startled.

"My friend," laughed Abu Said, "do not be so worried. The Pasha was so concerned about you managing to get the right quantity and quality of merchandise with which to bribe the Emir, that he let me into the secret. Don't worry - it is quite safe with me. Neither my Negro whipmaster nor my white page boys can understand Turkish. They will simply think that you have come into a fortune, or made a killing by investing in a highly successful

Corso. And as for me, just remember that although I also deal in horses and other animals, my whole livelihood would be jeopardised if the French landed and stopped the Corsairs from raiding the European coasts for women."

My mind eased. But even so the cost would be huge. I turned and looked at the three women. Indeed what a gift they would make for the Emir. They seemed almost too good to be true, as they silently stood there, their eyes downcast with shame. I could certainly see that these women might well be decisive in changing the loyalty of the Emir of Rebar - and hence, perhaps, to the whole future of the Barbary States.

"They only speak Swedish," said Abu Said. "Perhaps that is just as well. They will have no idea of the life that lies ahead of them - not even when you are marching them across the desert and scrub to the castle of the Emir."

He nodded to the huge Negro, who bent down and slowly raised the embroidered flap which hid the mother's intimacies.

Clearly she had just been shorn. But she had been only half shorn and there was no mistaking the natural golden colour of the hair in the little half circle that so prettily ringed her now shaven and exposed beauty lips.

She blushed deeply, clearly too embarrassed to say a word, and anyway doubtless aware that no one in Marsa understood a word of Swedish.

But that was not all.

The Negro raised the flap higher to expose her belly.

It was swollen!

"Yes, my friend," said Abu Said, "she is pregnant to her late lamented husband who was killed when his ship was boarded - he who sired these two beautiful daughters ... Now do you agree that they are very valuable?"

I had to admit that he had a point.

But still more was disclosed by the raising of the flap.

The mother had been cleverly infibulated.

A beautifully made little padlock had been fastened through her beauty lips. The metal that pierced them was hardly thicker than a needle. But attached to it were two short curved bars which ran up the side of the lips squeezing them together. I could see that until the padlock was unlocked there would be no possibility of even a

106

little finger penetrating between the lips, never mind some blunt instrument or a man's manhood.

And yet the permanent piercing of the inner lips was hardly visible, the holes were just large enough for the needle-like clasp of the padlock to be threaded through them.

The effect was to accentuate the now protruding and tightly squeezed lips from which the small padlock hung.

"With such a valuable merchandise," explained Abu Said, speaking again in Arabic, "one cannot risk an upset, whether it is self induced or the result of activity by others."

Matrak smiled in agreement. I had not known that they were friends, though chief black eunuchs are naturally known to slave dealers who regularly visit them to learn whether the eunuch's Master is thinking of acquiring more slave girls for his harem, or wants to reduce his stock. I remembered that Matrak had not seemed unduly worried about the new requirement to produce blond women for the Emir of Rebar's famous breeding establishment. Perhaps he had heard about this Swedish family. But I did not want to pry.

The Negro lowered the mother's flap and raised that of the youngest girl. She cried out "Mamma! Mamma!" and then quickly fell silent when the Negro raised his whip. She too blushed prettily, just as her mother had done.

She too had been infibulated like her mother, with a small padlock hanging down from the little pink inner lips.

Then the Negro moved to the older girl.

"Of course, for the two young girls, the padlock and the squeezing bars are to ensure their continuing virginity," said Abu Said, speaking in Turkish again. "You see I have thought of everything. Not only do I want to make sure that you can deliver the mother still carrying her child, but also that the two daughters do not become pregnant."

He looked me in the eyes and laughed.

"Nor do we want to risk them producing a half Irish dark haired brat! They are after all very attractive girls."

They were indeed. What a responsibility to ensure that they were not inadvertently covered on the march or in the training camp. Thank heavens they had been infibulated! Perhaps it would be as well to have the matched pairs that Abu Hussein was producing also infibulated to ensure nothing untoward happened.

But all that was for the future. I had to concentrate on the present - especially with so much at stake, financially and politically.

"May Matrak ..." I began to ask.

"Of course he can examine them. That's what they're here for. He will find them in perfect condition."

Matrak went up to the mother. The Negro whipmaster placed a little stool in front of the woman for him to sit on and then raised the flap again. Then Matrak ran his black hands over her full white breasts and down over her belly and hips. He was not interested in the woman's evident beauty, but only in her breeding capacity.

The whipmaster handed him a little key. Matrak gently unlocked the padlock. The woman looked down nervously, anxious to see what they were doing to her.

"Head up!" shouted the Negro whipmaster.

This must have been an order she had learnt to obey, for instantly she raised her head and looked straight forward. But then in an instinctive gesture of modesty she pressed her knees together.

"Legs apart!" shouted the whipmaster.

Again it must have been an order she had learnt to obey for with a little gasp of despair, she parted her legs, slightly bent her knees, and turned her ankles outwards - all the while keeping her eyes fixed ahead.

Matrak slowly removed the needle-like clasp of the padlock from her pierced body lips. As he did so, her body lips opened up like a flower. I saw Matrak part them. I heard the woman give another gasp, but she did not dare to look down or break position. I saw that she was biting her lips with discomfort and humiliation - for Matrak was always very thorough when inspecting a woman intimately.

Finally, he seemed satisfied. He nodded at his fellow Negro who was now holding the padlock and its two little flat bars. Whilst Matrak held the lips tightly closed again, the whipmaster threaded the clasp through the tiny perforations and then closed the padlock again with the key.

The woman was blushing with shame and embarrassment. To have two Negroes open up her intimacies, examine them and then close them up again, all in front of two other men and her own daughters, must have been terribly degrading. She would soon have to get used to being treated far worse than this.

Matrak and the whipmaster now repeated the process with the eldest daughter. She wriggled frantically in protest as she felt Matrak's hands touching her intimately. She started to cry out in Swedish. The whipmaster unfastened his whip from his belt and gave her a sharp stroke across her naked belly. She screamed but she kept quite still from then on.

It was interesting to see in this younger woman how the flowering effect, as the padlock was removed, was much less noticeable. Her lips remained quite well closed. This was a girl who had not yet carried a child and who, indeed, was still a virgin. It would soon be very different.

Matrak's investigation was more delicate and far less probing than with the mother. I could see that he was checking the girl's virginity as well as on her breeding capability. Since the profitability of the blond breeding farm largely depended on a high level of twins, the girl's ability to carry and successfully deliver twins would also effect her value. I saw that Matrak was accordingly feeling her hips carefully.

Then it was the turn of the youngest daughter, and the process was the same.

Matrak stood up and turned to me.

"They very suitable."

Abu Said's smile was huge. It was, I thought, almost as huge as the price would be. I knew I must buy them, whatever the cost.

He snapped his fingers. The Negro whipmaster drew the curtain back across the alcove, putting the women, still breathing heavily from their degrading experiences, back into darkness.

I could hear little whispers from the girls as they tremulously asked their mother what was happening. The whipmaster angrily pulled the curtain back slightly. His whip was raised.

"Silence!" he shouted. There was no doubting his meaning. He let the curtain fall again. There was now complete silence from behind it.

"Let us have some coffee," said Abu Said.

I was now in for some long and difficult bargaining.

"I'm not sure I need all of them," I said to Abu Said, lying as was expected of me by this wily Oriental trader. "However, you will probably not wish to split them, so ..."

CHAPTER 21 - THE TRAINING CAMP

I dismissed my personal guard of Janissaries.

Then, with Tulip, I rode up the hill to the small white painted fort as I had done early every morning since completing my purchases a month previously. The Pasha wanted us to move out shortly and the girls were almost ready.

The fort was square shaped. It was no longer used to guard the approach to Marsa and had become abandoned. Recently it had been used periodically by the Pasha as a base for hunting. Inside the walls there was just an empty sandy arena and several large cages, built specially by the Pasha for hunting dogs and cheetahs. The sandy arena and the cages made it ideal for my purpose.

As I approached the fort, the detachment of a dozen of the Pasha's own Black Guard turned out to salute me. They had been detailed to guard the fort and its secret inmates.

Not all the detachment were Dinka giants like the two who had flogged Madame de Savoury and her maid during their interrogation in the Pasha's dungeons. Those two had been sent here to act as slave drivers for my two coffles.

It was important, of course, that whilst being responsible for guarding the delightful contents of the fort, the Black Guards did not have access to them. The Pasha and I had therefore decided that the Black Guards should remain outside the fort itself.

It was, of course, true that whilst I had been away in the interior looking for Madame de Savoury, Matrak had had the girls of the display team and one of my stirrup girls covered by the two Dinka slave drivers. But this had been intended and had been carefully planned and supervised.

The Black Guards were lined up smartly under the orders of their sergeant. They presented arms. It had been an interesting experience, first smartening up the Janissaries, the white troops, and then using one of their drill sergeants to smarten the Pasha's Black Guards.

There was considerable rivalry between the two military units, though their roles were quite different. The Janissaries, of course, provided the armed landing parties and the boarding parties for the Corso. They also enabled the various Deys and Beys of the Barbary Ports to keep order amongst the Berber tribes immediately surrounding them - and to extract taxes from them. The Black Guards of the Pasha of Marsa, like those of the Sultan of Morocco, were his personal bodyguard. They were also used for certain secret missions on which it might be imprudent to use the Janissaries - like guarding the fort whilst it was being used as a female training camp.

Whilst the Janissaries were nominally the slaves of the Sultan in far away Constantinople, the Black Guards were the actual slaves of the Pasha of Marsa.

To ensure greater secrecy for the enterprise, this detachment of Black Guards would not be allowed back to Marsa until after I had set off inland with my coffles of white women. I had anticipated that this would cause resentment. I had, therefore, used a little of the gold from the Pasha's purse to increase their food and pay whilst they were guarding the fort.

The heavy iron studded doors of the fort opened and I rode into the fort with Tulip riding behind me. I was greeted by Matrak and the Dinka slave drivers. With them was one of the Pasha's Negro grooms whom he had sent to train the display team and stirrup girls and then act as slave driver on the march. They had all left their charges in the care of their young Negro assistants. These boys would also be coming on the march and would be mounted, as befitted an overseer, however young. So including my own two horses, and a spare horse for the others, and other spare horses for Matrak and Tulip, I reckoned we would need about ten or a dozen horses. The women would each have to carry a heavy weight of food, merely to feed us and our horses - never mind themselves.

I had thought of leaving Tulip behind, but the Pasha had insisted that I should take him to lend more dignity to myself. Moreover, the Pasha had added, if I did not travel with a garzon, as these page boys were euphemistically called, then the tribal leaders would suspect that I had used the girls for my manly needs and would regard them as used goods.

As Matrak and his slave drivers bowed, I saw that my two stirrup girls were prostrating themselves humbly on the sand behind them.

The first one was that little minx Beatriz, the young wife of a Portuguese sea captain, whom I had bought after her brave little show of temper. Despite Abu Said's foreboding, the combined whips of the Negro groom, and of Matrak, seemed to have tamed her. She followed me around like a little dog when I was in the fort, never taking her eyes off me. This, of course was how she was supposed to behave as a stirrup running girl, but it only made me lust after her all the more.

The other was the buxom Italian convent girl whom I had bought as a stirrup girl after watching her being aroused by her Negro overseer in the slave market of Tal Basr. Matrak had her covered by the Dinkas whilst I was away in the interior, and her belly was now beginning to swell with the black child she was carrying. Like the girls of the display team she had been deliberately mated with both of the Dinkas to prevent her forming a sentimental attachment to one of them as the sire of her progeny. Instead, as befitted a stirrup girl, she had clearly fallen in love with me!

Like the other girls in the fort, both my stirrup girls were naked except for their heavy black cotton mesh muzzles and their green cotton trousers. To harden their feet for the march they were kept barefoot.

The muzzles also acted as a veil covering the girl's face below her eyes. They would help to disguise the European origin of the slaves, when they were not wearing their long white bakras or shrouds. But the muzzles were also intended to discourage the girls from talking, and to prevent them from eating more than their ration of food. This would be particularly important on the march, where in their hunger they might try to snatch berries and roots, or even the oats for the horses. In either case we did not want to risk any stomach upsets. The muzzles were only removed at the daily feeding time.

The thin cotton trousers were fastened with a cord high up round the waist, above the swelling bellies of the pregnant girls. They were tight round the legs, but were completely cut away in front, prettily displaying the girls' navels, bellies and beauty lips. This was an erotic sight that I felt would be much appreciated by the unsophisticated tribal leaders of the interior.

CHAPTER 22 - A LITTLE TRAINING

Matrak led the way up one of the corner towers of the fort where under the shade of an awning he kept his records. From there he could look down into the courtyard and see everything that was going on.

The two stirrup girls followed me adoringly, each carrying a ceremonial parasol, with which they shielded me from the now mild autumnal sun. This was all part of their training - to follow me everywhere when I was outside, whether I was mounted or not, and always keeping their parasols over my head. It was, I had to admit, a very satisfying little attention. It was very good for one's ego to have two beautiful and half naked girls struggling to keep the merest glimmer of a sun's ray off one's face.

I sat down on a comfortable cushion and sipped cool and refreshing sherbet whilst Matrak made his usual report about the state of each girl. I was glad to hear that none of them had yet guessed what was in store for them. Down in the courtyard was a scene of activity as each coffle was put through its paces by its slave driver. Only the precious blond breeding team were absent. They were Matrak's personal responsibility in view of their value and were still in their cage.

I initialled Matrak's records and went down into the sand covered courtyard with him. My two stirrup girls ran behind us, keeping their parasols raised over my head as I went over to where one of the coffles was being exercised.

I was rather proud of the system of coffles that I had finally adopted. Coffles were, of course, needed not only to prevent any of the girls from trying to escape, but also to prevent any marauding Arabs from stealing any of them.

At first I had assumed that we would simply use the same system as the slavers who brought coffles of Negresses across the Sahara. They simply chained the women by the neck one behind the other. But this seemed very dull and unimaginative. I wanted something that would really show off my beautiful white slaves. Moreover, having taken a lot of trouble to divide the women into matched pairs, I wanted to highlight this aspect.

I smiled approvingly at the first coffle. Seven pairs of girls, led by their lead girl, were running round their arena behind a young black boy, their apprentice slave driver, who was riding a well groomed Arab horse. Their Dinka slave driver himself was standing up on a small podium in the center of the arena, a long carriage whip in his hand. The women were sweating profusely, but they were not puffing and blowing as they had a month previously: they were now much fitter.

Each girl carried a large pack on her back, supported by straps going over her shoulders from a tight belt fastened round her waist just above the cord of her trousers. The packs would be used to carry food for the horses and ourselves during the march - in this way, the girls would serve as our pack animals. For the time being the packs were simply filled with stones. At first the girls had been exercised with loads of only twenty pounds, but they were now getting used to carrying a full forty pounds.

To prevent the straps from chafing their nipples, they were crossed over between the breasts before being fastened again to the side of the belt. It was of course very much in each girl's interests to keep her harness soft and well oiled so that it did not rub her body.

The lead girl of this coffle was the delightful buxom girl I had specially bought as a lead girl at the Tal Basr slave market when looking for Madame de Savoury. She now looked well muscled as she trotted behind the boy's horse. A length of light chain went from his hand to the ring in front of the girl's well polished brass collar. She was the only girl in her coffle to be collared.

Another length of chain, this time a good deal heavier, went from the ring on the back of her collar to a ring halfway along the front of a hinged plank or yoke that held the necks of the first matched pair. It was some four feet long and over a foot wide. It was a substantial looking piece of wood, some two inches thick. The yoke was in two halves with a hinge at one end to enable it to be opened. At the other end was a locking bolt for keeping it securely closed. Each half had two semi-circular holes forming, when the two halves were closed together, two round holes.

Inside the holes, some three feet apart, were the necks of the girls of the first matched pair.

The effect was striking: it was as if two pretty little heads that had just been struck off by the headsman's axe and placed on the plank. But the heads were alive! It was an effect only partly spoilt by the two pairs of naked breasts that jutted out just below the plank.

The timber yoke that held the first matched couple was linked to that of the next pair by a sturdy six foot long chain fastened to a ring at the back of the first pair's yoke, and to a ring on the front of the yoke of the second pair. These rings were halfway between the two girls' pretty heads. A similar chain linked them to the next matched pair and so on.

To encourage each pair to behave more and more like one entity, they would be kept locked within their yoke until they were given away to their new Master. Even then, I felt, it was likely that their delighted Master might well continue to keep his newly acquired pair coupled up together in this erotic way.

The six foot separation between the couples was intended to allow each to lie down on their backs at night or when resting, one behind the other, scooping a little sand to make a pillow to relieve the pressure of the plank on the backs of their necks.

The sight of these matched pairs prancing along behind their slave driver's horses, their naked breasts bouncing, their soft bellies displayed by their cutaway trousers and their hairless beauty lips so prominent, was indeed an erotic sight. It would, I was sure, drive the tribal leaders into a frenzy.

But I had decided on yet another little touch: guide chains.

To help each pair act and move as one, the inside wrists of each pair, that is to say the left wrist of the right hand girl and the right wrist of the left hand girl, were closely manacled together. Hanging from the manacles were little bells which rang with their every movement.

I still wanted to give greater cohesiveness to the coffle as a whole, especially when it was moving at speed, or changing direction. Therefore, remembering how teams of stage coach horses were harnessed together to achieve the same effect, I had arranged for a light chain to be fastened to a manacle on the lead girl's belled right wrist. This lead back to the right wrist of the right hand girl of the first pair, and then back along the lines of pairs, linking all the right wrists of the right hand girls. Similarly, a light chain linked the lead girl's left wrist back to the left wrists of the left hand girls of each pair.

In this way, if, for instance, the coffle had to wheel to the left behind their slave driver's horse, then the lead girl could pull on her right wrist to speed up the right hand girls and thus ensure that each pair in the coffle wheeled in succession to the left exactly in the hoof marks of the horse.

Seeing my approach the slave driver called out an order to his boy apprentice, who immediately started to ride the horse on a complicated zig-zag course around various stone markers in the arena. It was fascinating to see how the long snake of the coffle weaved its way around behind the horse and the lead girl, who was alternatively signalling down the line first with one wrist chain and then the other.

It was particularly fascinating to see how the pairs all ran in step with all the two inner legs of each pair moving together, and all the two outer legs of each pair also striking the ground together in perfect time.

It was something that had taken hours of practice, and much use of the slave driver's whip, to perfect.

The slave driver now called out a preparatory order. Nothing happened. Then he cracked his whip loudly. All the girls of the coffle took two more paces and then as one started to raise their knees high in the air, until their thighs were perfectly horizontal, before they were dropped again to the vertical. I saw that the locked wooden planks were all thrust back as the girls leaned back slightly as they strained to maintain their now high stepping action, weaving to and fro around the arena. The prancing action was, of course, particularly hard work to achieve whilst also carrying a forty pound pack on their backs!

It was an excellent exercise for the girl's thigh, stomach and back muscles. At first, they could only keep it up for a few minutes. Now, with a certain amount of encouragement from their slave driver's whip, they could manage ten minutes or more, though the sweat would soon be running down between their breasts.

The prancing step was something I felt that the inland leaders would be fascinated with. It would be performed as we arrived at his castle, or kasbah, and entered the courtyard.

Normally when on the march the slave driver might well lead the coffle on his own horse, leaving the young black boy to ride up and down the line, using the whip to keep the coffle moving at a smart trot. But when approaching a castle he would certainly be riding up and down the line himself ensuring that the coffle was keeping perfect step and prancing properly when ordered to do so.

This Dinka already has his coffle already well trained. I strode over to the other.

They were practising quickly putting on and taking off the all enveloping white shrouds which went over their heads, through the neck coffle holes in the wooden planks and on down to their bare feet. A little cotton mesh grill allowed them to see out.

The shrouds would be worn when the sun was particularly hot, so as to keep the bodies nice and white for the inspection of the tribal leaders. They would also disguise the fact that they were captured Europeans and not merely local Berber girls captured in some inter-tribal feuding. The girls' muzzles would also act sufficiently as a veil to deceive a casual passing Arab traveller. The shrouds would be removed as we approached the castle of a particular leader, so as to ensure his greater interest.

The shrouds could be rolled up and fastened at the back of each plank. To put them on or off, the matched pairs would close up to give their chained hands more freedom, with each pair helping the pair in front of them, the front pair helping the lead girl, and the black boy helping the rear pair. It was a drill that they had learned to carry out quickly to their slave driver's order.

It was then feeding time. This formed an important part of their training, for on the march they would have to eat only the boiled barley and oats that they carried on their backs for the horses, mixed with a few dates.

One advantage of this parsimonious diet was that there was little risk of the girls putting on any unnecessary weight. This particularly applied to the pregnant display girls, and to my own stirrup girls. They would remain attractively slim and thus all the better show off their swelling lower bellies and breasts.

On the march, of course, there would be no troughs for the girls to eat out of. Therefore, here in the training camp, they had to learn to guzzle up their food off the sandy, gritty and often muddy and dung covered ground. This also helped give them the necessary

117

minerals that they might not otherwise have received. It had taken their bellies a little time to adjust to such a diet. However, in extremis, on the march they might well have to be fed on cakes baked from dried horse and camel dung. It was therefore important to accustom them to it.

I saw the girls' heads turning in their planks to eye with a ravenous look the large bowl that their black apprentice boy was bringing. It contained a sort of porridge made from oats and barley. I saw him add a little salt to give it more taste: salt was an important food in the interior. I saw him bend down to scoop up a little dried horse dung, together with the sand and grit on which it had been laying. He added a few dates do give the girls a little something to scramble for. It was not a mixture that appealed to me, but then I was not a ravenously hungry young slave girl.

He threw two dollops of the mixture down onto the ground between each matched pair and one in front of the lead girl, then gave an order. Again it was only a preparatory one and nothing happened. This was a technique I wholeheartedly approved of as a way of disciplining women. Then he clapped his hands and instantly each matched pair fell to their knees and started desperately to guzzle up the mixture. With their outside hands half tied by the guide chains, and their inner ones tightly manacled together, most of the food was eaten by the girls immersing their faces in the mixture.

It was just at that moment that Matrak came up to me to invite me to go over and see the display team being drilled, and then go on and see the blond breeding slaves in their cage.

"I have a little surprise for you, Effendi," he said.

CHAPTER 23 - THE SURPRISE

The two lines of the display team were facing each other, each five strong with its own lead girl on the right of the line. A heavy log was being lifted off the ground by one line. The team was crouching down. Each girl's wrists were manacled to those of the girl on either side of her. Thus, ten hands were being driven to lift the heavy log. The team's Negro boy was going down the line feeling the girls' arm and shoulder muscles to make sure that each was really straining.

The big Negro slave driver, the groom that the Pasha had specially sent me to train and supervise this team, cracked his whip. There was a pause and then the whole line slowly straightened their legs, lifting the log as they stood up. They lifted it up past their swelling bellies and held it up level with their breasts for a full minute. Then, in response to another crack of the whip, they slowly passed it to the other line, facing them.

The second line also held it up for a minute until the whip cracked again, whereupon they slowly bent their knees and lowered the log to the ground. The whip then cracked again, and the whole process recommenced.

I could see the strain on the women's faces as they gritted their teeth under the heavy weight.

They had been doing this exercise for a quarter of an hour. It was an excellent exercise for pregnant women. It was also an excellent way of making the whole line work as one team, taking their time from their lead girl.

I was pleased to see how buxom the girls were becoming. This was, of course, nature's response to the fact that they had been crossed with Dinka giants. The progeny now growing in them would be exceptionally large and would need, at birth, a good deal more milk than a normal white baby.

The name Display Team was perhaps a misnomer. With their swollen bellies and heavy progeny, they would not be expected to run behind my horse in the same prancing step as the coffles of matched pairs. Nor would they be used as pack animals like the matched pairs. No, it was their pretty protruding bellies that were on display. These were beautifully outlined by their cut away trousers, which had a gold lace edge to the cut away to give further emphasis to the curve of the belly.

Tulip brought out my horse. Its tack had been changed, and it now carried my beautifully fringed red leather ceremonial bridle and reins. The slave driver gave an order. Obediently, the two lines formed up behind me.

The Negro boy started to harness the women. A fringed red leading rein went back from each of my stirrups to the collars of the two girls on either end of the first line. Two more matching, but shorter, fringed red leading reins went from the ring on the back of each outside girl's collar, back to the ring on the collars of the outside girls of the second line. The lines now locked together and could be wheeled and manoeuvred by me by pushing one stirrup forward, and the other back. I could also signal an increase in speed by pushing both stirrups forward.

To ensure that each line was kept perfectly aligned, a light pole, painted to match the remainder of the harness, had been passed through the rings at the back of the collar of each girl in the line.

The boy now went down the two lines, unclipping each girl's wrist manacle from that of her neighbour, and instead clipping them both together behind her back. This thrust their breasts forward, displaying them even better. On the march they would normally be allowed to have their wrists clipped to those of the next girl, but arriving at the Castle of a chieftain, they would quickly be fastened behind their backs, as at present, for the ceremonial arrival.

The sight of all this was quite dramatic, as the pregnant young women, attractively harnessed together, were made to run in step, in two perfectly straight lines, behind my horse. It was a sight that would really emphasise to the tribal rulers what they could expect in future, if they remained loyal to the Sultan.

The slave driver beckoned to my stirrup girls. They too were now fastened to my stirrups on either side of my horse by similar red fringed leading reins that were attached to the rings on the front of their shiny brass collars.

The Negro slave driver looked at the women to check that they were all correctly harnessed, then nodded at me. My display team and stirrup running girls were ready to be exercised.

Whilst Tulip held my horse, I mounted. As I thrust my feet into the well polished stirrups, I could feel the tension in the leading reins going back to the display team. I also felt the shade of the two parasols held up over my head by my stirrup girls.

Tulip released the bridle. My horse began to move forward. I touched him with my spurs, whilst keeping him well reined back. Well schooled, he started to canter slowly, whilst remaining virtually on the spot. The display team started to run slowly behind my prancing horse in perfect response.

For the next half hour, I trotted around the sandy arenas that made up the inside of the fort, twisting and turning and steering both my display team and my stirrup girls around a complex course. Soon I was joined by the two coffles of matched pairs, with their slave drivers riding horses behind the display team.

All that was missing was our special coffle of blond breeding women. They were, of course, highly valuable and warranted individual care and attention, far too valuable to be used as pack animals. But they would still have to be fit enough to take their place in the line of slave women, between the two coffles of matched pairs. After a time, therefore, Matrak went back to their cage and brought them out to join us.

It was important that their blond hair should at all times on the march be hidden from the sight of other passing travellers or potential brigands. Therefore, as well as their cutaway trousers, and their muzzles, they also wore a black chador that covered the tops of their heads. They were simply chained together by the neck one behind the other. To a casual observer, they would be just another group of slave women being taken inland.

Suddenly as they passed me on their way to take up their allocated place, I was astonished to see that instead of the usual three figures, the Swedish mother and her two daughters, there were now four, half hidden beneath their chadors and muzzles.

"The Pasha say," called out Matrak as he marched the group past me, "blond breeding women should have own lead girl, already broken into slavery. He send girl from own harem. She very pretty. Very valuable too. Pasha say he only send her because our mission so important. He say you keep her as special bargaining power with Emir of Rebar. If you not need give her to him, then he want her back again in harem."

He cracked his whip and they started to run round one of the arenas. Since they were intended to be kept hidden until we arrived at the castle of the Emir of Rebar, and then only shown to him discreetly to wet his appetite, there was no need to train them to prance. They would just have to run along in the middle of the long line of women with, above all, their blond hair hidden from sight.

The new lead girl led the line. Encouraged by Matrak's whip, she was setting a fast pace. Behind her ran the two slighter figure of the two Swedish daughters. I could see that they were watching

121

Matrak's whip with alarm. Behind them came their mother with her naked belly nicely swollen to show off her interesting state - a state that, doubtlessly, would greatly interest the Emir when he learned that the sire was not one of the Pasha's Dinka giants but the woman's own Swedish husband, the sire of her two blond, blue eyed, beautiful daughters.

Matrak halted the women. He was not satisfied with them. He barked a word of command. The four women now all held out their right arms straight, at an angle of forty five degrees to their bodies. Matrak went down the line, checking that each girl's arm was held at just the right angle and that her feet were exactly on either side of a line drawn in the sand so that they lined up perfectly.

Then he produced a wrist coffle, went to the lead girl, and snapped the manacle round her right wrist. Keeping her head up and looking straight in front of her, the lead girl then smartly dropped her arm and smacked her outstretched hand against her thigh. Matrak went to the next girl and snapped a manacle round her wrist. She too then smacked her arm against her thigh. Matrak continued down the line and then repeated the process with their left wrists. The blond breeding women were now chained in a line, not only by the neck, but also by both wrists. This would be the normal situation on the march. I could not risk anyone stealing one of them.

Matrak gave a word of command. Immediately the women, all stepping off with the left foot, resumed their fast run, their breasts swinging and their now chained wrists moving to and fro in perfect unison.

There was something rather familiar about the lead girl. Was it the way she held herself, half naked in the cutaway trousers, or the hang of her breasts, or her slim straight legs?

Her belly, displayed by her cutaway green trousers, was deliciously soft, but flat. Nor were there any stretch marks from previous pregnancies. Neither situation was likely to remain for long once the Emir of Rebar had her in his breeding farm - if indeed I did have to offer her to the Emir to clinch the renewal of his loyalty to the Sultan.

She had a beautiful figure. No wonder the Pasha wanted her back, if I did not have to use her. It certainly showed how serious he was taking the Emir of Rebar that he could have brought himself to part with such a delightful creature.

Matrak halted them to give them a breather. Their naked breasts were rising and falling fast with exertion.

I rode over to them.

"You like see new blond girl, I think," said Matrak. He unfastened the lead girl's muzzle that veiled her face and slipped her black chador down over her neck.

The beautiful features of Mrs. Henrietta Hamilton stared up at me.

I was astonished.

"You!"

It was all I could find to say to the young woman who for months had hardly been out of my thoughts.

She blushed furiously, and with her chained hands tried ineffectually to cover her naked breasts and her exposed beauty lips.

"You! The Englishman!" she said in a horse whisper, her eyes staring in disbelief.

There was a sudden rattle of the chains that held her wrists to those of her companions. I glanced down. She was no longer trying to hide her charms, but rather the brand on her belly that was so prominently displayed by her cutaway trousers, immediately above her gleaming infibulation ring. It was a brand that was intended constantly to remind the Emir of Rebar, once the girl was safely incarcerated in the pens and cages of his blond breeding farm, just how far the Pasha was willing to go to retain his allegiance.

But for the moment the girl was simply trying to hide from me the brand that for the rest of her life would show that she had once been the trained concubine of the Pasha of Marsa! It was the instinctive gesture of a woman trying to hide from the eyes of a new and potentially jealous lover, the outward signs of her former life.

It showed that my interest in her was returned - even if equally hopelessly.

CHAPTER 24 - A STALLION SLAVE

"As you can see," said Mahmud with a laugh, "there is still plenty of demand for a pretty boy in Marsa."

It was Friday, the Moslem Sabbath day. We were strolling across the main square opposite the principal mosque on our way to Mahmud's establishment, where I had arranged to have a discreet look at the goods currently in stock.

I felt sick at heart. It was only two days after the shattering discovery of Henrietta amongst the girls in the fort. My instinctive reaction would normally have been to have her released from her coffle and brought to me for my enjoyment. I had, after all, lusted after her for months. Like a love-sick boy, I had constantly worried and wondered about her - the only English woman I had ever come across in Marsa. The knowledge that the Pasha had her locked up in his harem had driven me half mad with jealousy. Every time I met the Pasha I would ask myself if he had just come from her arms.

I did not of course discuss Henrietta with the Pasha, other than thanking him for making up the numbers in the coffle of the blond breeding women. He had merely grunted in reply. She was merely a slave. It would have been unseemly to mention her by name. Moslem men did not discuss their former concubines with each other.

Somehow, I controlled my desires. Somehow I managed to keep away from the small coffle of blond women of which Henrietta was now the lead girl. Somehow, I had managed to keep my face a mask as Matrak reported on her progress.

So near and yet so far!

It was no wonder that my mind was in a turmoil as I walked across the crowded square with Mahmud. He was a friendly young man, with the reputation of having made a fortune out of supplying one of Marsa's most important needs.

Traditionally, this was the day when men who kept a team of garzons, as young boy concubines were called, proudly paraded through the streets followed by their richly attired and heavily painted boys and youths. During the week they were as closely guarded as the most beautiful female concubines, but on Fridays their owners enjoyed showing them off to their admiring, and often jealous, friends.

Two heavily bearded grave-faced merchants, deep in conversation, passed us, greeting Mahmud politely. Clearly they had often done business with him. Each was followed by a couple of prettily made-up white youths wearing silken trousers and short waistcoats. They flashed their eyes unashamedly at us behind their Master's backs.

"The fact is," said Mahmud, "keeping one or two garzons for one's manly needs is often simpler and more practical for a man, especially if he does a lot of travelling."

Mahmud was quite right of course. In a society in which both respectable women and slave girls are kept veiled and locked up out of sight, the advantage of having a garzon was considerable. I remembered how, for instance, the Pasha had insisted that I should take Tulip with me on my forthcoming expedition into the interior. The idea of taking a castrated page boy with me, when in theory I had Henrietta at my beck and call, made it even more ironic.

The boys following the two merchants walked with almost the same swaying motion of a girl, and that under their waistcoats were the signs of budding little breasts.

We momentarily entered a barber's shop. Perfumed young white boys, naked except for a little flap of cloth hanging from their waists, were trimming the beards of the patrons, who were themselves discussing amongst themselves the rival attractions of the boys attending on them, before deciding to hire the services of one or more of them for an hour or two in a private room.

"And is there no requirement, these days, for uncut young white men?" I asked conversationally, as we left the barber's shop. I knew the answer before Mahmud spoke.

"Not really. They are too much trouble and not worth while owning now that there is no demand for male galley slaves in the sea-going corsair ships. Owners of the inshore galliots, farms, carpet factories and mills have all learned to use white female slaves. Not only are they easier to break and train, but they can also be used to reward their Negro overseers for increasing production - and thus also produce a useful annual cash crop of mulatto slaves into the bargain. So no one really wants to be bothered with troublesome young males. When the corsairs do

125

capture any, then they are usually thrown overboard or released. But there is, of course, one exception."

"Oh?" I said.

"Yes," said the slaver, "there is a demand for good looking young aristocrats. Perhaps spurred by the recent revolution in France, it amuses a rich Moslem to have a foppish young European aristocrat as a personal slave. And, of course, they can usually be ransomed for a high price. But even then, they are usually gelded to prevent any trouble. Of course," Mahmud added with a laugh, "they don't tell the young man's family that their precious young offspring has been cut!"

"And the breeders?" I asked with forced nonchalance. I did not want Mahmud to know my real reason for visiting his establishment was to see if by chance he had a blond boy whom I could offer the Emir of Rebar for his blond breeding farm. Let him go on thinking that the boy was for myself! "Do they not want to buy grown men for use in their slave breeding farms?"

"Not usually," replied Mahmud. "A breeder prefers to buy a good looking blond haired boy, if he can get one, and then try him out on one or two slave girls. If the offsprings are suitable, then he will keep the boy and use him for many years. If the progeny are no good, then he can have the boy gelded and sell him as a garzon so as to get his money back. A really good stallion boy can be used again and again."

No wonder, I thought, that Abu Said had been so convinced that the Emir of Rebar would be so excited by being offered a Swedish mother and with two daughters and another on the way. It would save him years of patient work in rebuilding his distinctive strain. And, I thought with a sickening feeling, Henrietta could provide the progeny for outcrossing to a different strain.

We had now arrived at Mahmud's establishment. It was surrounded, of course, by a well guarded high wall, both to prevent his slaves from escaping and to prevent robbers from breaking in and stealing his valuable stock of captured Christian boys.

A black servant came up to him and whispered in his ear.

"Ah!" said Mahmud turning to me. "A display is just starting. Come along and we'll watch. This is something rather different, a little unusual."

126

Intrigued, I followed him up some stairs and into a corridor. He pointed to a screen of latticed wood. It was similar to the ones in my own house through which I could look down unobserved into my harem. I looked through it.

Half a dozen naked youths were standing on a long platform.

"Shush!" said Mahmud. "Here come the prospective buyers."

I had expected to see bearded men. I was therefore astonished to see two veiled women come into the room, followed at a distance by a third. They seemed like two wealthy women, attended by a slave girl.

"They are very rich," whispered Mahmud. "One is the widow of a merchant and the other the much indulged wife of another merchant. Women such as these form an important, but very discreet, part of my clientele and they often recommend me to their friends. To avoid any embarrassment, I always allow them to examine the wares alone." He winked. Clearly the women had no idea that they were being observed.

I heard the women's voices. They spoke with educated accents.

"Mahmud has certainly offered us a good selection this time," said one, throwing back her veil. I saw that she was an attractive, if hard looking, woman perhaps still in her late twenties. Her companion also threw back her veil. She was older, but still good looking, perhaps about forty. She must be the rich widow, I thought, and the other the indulged wife. The servant girl standing to one side remained veiled.

They began to feel and stroke the youths. Five of them were dark eyed and Italian looking, the sixth blond. There seemed something familiar about him.

As they went down the line feeling, probing and stroking, the youths began to writhe in their chains. Their long hair was stroked. The texture of their skins were compared. Their teeth were looked at. Their muscles were felt. And their manhoods were inspected closely.

I saw that the manhoods of those who had been gelded were beginning to react just like those who had not yet been cut. It was a sign, of course, that they had been gelded after puberty.

The two women gave the servant girl an order, and she too thrust back her veil. I saw that she was an outstandingly pretty girl,

French looking. What a waste, I thought, such beauty in the service of a woman rather than of a man.

She dropped her long black shroud. Under it she was stark naked. I gasped at her voluptuous figure, her large firm breasts, her tiny waist and her generous hips. Such a slave girl would have fetched a high price on the block.

The older woman, clearly her Mistress, gave her another order, in a sharp tone of voice. The girl turned towards the line of youths, then stepped up to the first in the line. She looked lovingly into his eyes. She rubbed her breasts against him. She rotated her belly against his. She kissed him on the mouth, at first daintily and then passionately. Her hand went down to touch his manhood.

Then after a moment she stood back. The boy's manhood was now revealed in its full rampant size.

Delighted, the older woman gripped it.

"Oh yes!" she cried. "This one is certainly vital, even if he has been gelded."

"And, of course," said the younger woman, "he will be able to give you hours of pleasure without spoiling it all by climaxing. None of the disappointing quick climaxes you so often get with a man."

She laughed. "Who would suspect such pleasure could come from a mere white eunuch! My fool of a husband has let me buy several. He just assumes that they were all castrated before puberty, like his black eunuchs, and are therefore quite harmless. But I can't tell you what pleasure I have had from them without once incurring any jealousy from my husband. My dear, you just don't know what excitements you'll now be able to buy for yourself as a rich woman."

The older woman laughed, and the naked girl started to arouse the next boy, who had not yet been gelded. The girl had to cut short her ministrations to prevent a sudden climax.

"If you choose one that has not yet been gelded," said the younger woman with a knowledgeable air, "then you can always attend the operation so that he associates his gelding with you. Thus, despite himself, as the effects of his castration become increasingly apparent, he will also increasingly become your devoted body slave."

"Body slave!" cried the older woman. "Yes that's what I want. And I'd certainly like him to be looking helplessly into my eyes as the knife did its work." She paused. "But if I do buy one that has not yet been castrated, can I be sure that he will still be virile after he has been cut?"

"Oh it makes no difference, provided it is done after puberty. And anyway, Mahmud would always take back a boy you were dissatisfied with. He can easily sell him to a man. Men don't want their page boys to be virile, if they are to attend on them when they are visiting their harems!"

"Yes, I see," said the older woman with a gleam in her eye.

All six of the youths, both those gelded and those still uncut, were now rampant. The older woman went down the line again, feeling and stroking.

"These Christian dogs seem so different, not having cut like a true believer," she said.

"I can assure you," laughed the younger woman, "that that gives a woman even more pleasure. Sometimes I regret that cutting is part of our religion."

The older woman nodded and stood back looking at the boys on display.

"It's so difficult to make up my mind which one I want. Perhaps I'll take one that's already been gelded and one that I will have gelded - perhaps that blond one, though he's very expensive, I know. But I think he'd be worth it - if only to show off to my friends. Yes, I think I'll take him anyway ..."

As she talked, I suddenly realised why the blond boy seemed familiar. But it couldn't be true! Quickly I turned to Mahmud.

"That blond boy. Where did you get him? Is he Swedish?"

"How did you guess?" laughed Mahmud. "He was captured when two corsair ships boarded a Swedish merchant ship. One ship took some captured women and the other this young man. When I acquired him he told me that the other women had been his mother and sisters. I tried to find out what had happened to them, for many men would pay a small fortune to have such a team in their harems. Mere mothers and daughters, and sisters and brothers can both fetch very high prices, never mind this complete family, and blond to boot. Quite apart from what certain rich men would pay to have them in their harem, think of their value to the owner of a newly formed blond breeding farm!"

Yes indeed, I thought.

He shook his head sadly. "But alas, I was quite unable to trace the rest of his family. They must have been sold secretly. So I am just having to sell the boy by himself."

Then he looked at me curiously. "Surely you aren't interested? I would have thought that, being from Northern Europe yourself, you'd be more interested in those lovely dark-eyed Italian boys."

"No, I like blondes," I lied nonchalantly. I knew that I must not disclose the real reason why I wanted this one. Obviously he was the son of the Swedish woman I was going to give to the Emir of Rebar, and the brother of the two girls. It was an incredible discovery - and an incredible opportunity too.

"So I am very interested," I added, my voice rising with my suppressed excitement.

"Shush, Effendi! Keep your voice down. These women would be horrified if they discovered we had been watching them. Think of my reputation, please!"

"Very well, but what do you want for that Swedish boy in an uncut state?" I asked.

"Uncut? But surely you would want him gelded. You have a harem. He might usurp your privileges there!"

"Uncut!" I repeated.

Mahmud looked down into the display room.

"I think you are just too late," he smiled. "Our widow has made up her mind to take him. Blond boys are very popular with the ladies."

It was now or never.

"I will give you twenty per cent more than your asking price," I said. "But you must agree now. You must send down to the widow and tell her that the boy has been withdrawn from the sale."

Mahmud hesitated for a second. This was a most unexpected development.

"You have the money?" he asked anxiously. Turkish officers are not well paid.

I produced the Pasha's bag of gold, or rather what was left of it. It was enough.

"Done!" said Mahmud. We shook hands, for European customs had spread amongst the merchants in Marsa.

CHAPTER 25 - ON THE MARCH

I looked down the line of coffled women. The sight gave me a feeling of extraordinary power. I could feel my loins stirring in response.

The sun was getting up. We had marched, or rather trotted, all night with just a short rest every hour. By marching by night, by the light of the moon, we avoided being seen by other travellers. It was now nearly time to make camp and lie up for the day.

It was two weeks since we had slipped out of the fort during the night to avoid our departure being noticed. We had now covered a fair distance. I was glad that the Pasha had insisted on spending so much time getting the women really fit for this march.

I glanced at the distant line of mountains. I could see the pass that allowed the way through them. I could also just make out the castle of the Emir of Tatra that guarded the pass and enabled him to exact a toll from all who used it. His large coffee and cotton plantations must lie in the fertile ground at the foot of the mountains. He would be the first tribal leader I would be contacting, the first I would be bribing back to allegiance to the Sultan.

I was riding along at a gentle trot - a hound jog we would have called it back in Ireland. It was a speed that the women in the coffles could now maintain for long periods, both those yoked together in the lines of matched pairs and carrying a heavy load on their backs, and those running tight behind me in the display team carrying a steadily growing mulatto child in their bellies.

I glanced at the rear woman in that coffle, the Swedish mother. Her cutaway trousers were displaying her swollen belly well, though it was now noticeable that the shape was less prominent and more gently rounded than those in the display team who were carrying half Dinka giants.

I looked at the figure running behind her. Her son! He too was chained to the coffle by the neck and by his wrists. His blond hair too was hidden, by a simple turban. He too wore the same cutaway trousers as the women.

My eyes went to Henrietta at the head of the coffle. I saw her blush as I looked down at her cutaway trousers and at her exposed beauty lips glistening under the little moustache that Matrak was now making her grow. She had, of course, been as hairless as a baby when she had arrived from the Pasha's harem.

With these thoughts racing through my mind, I finally glanced at my two stirrup girls, running at my side. They had pulled their long parasols from out of the cases that were slung over their shoulders, and were taking it in turn to shield me from the rising sun. It was a task that required concentration and dedication.

They were both looking up at me with adoration - as was proper in a stirrup slave. Their bellies were also now showing well in their cutaway trousers. They would certainly make a striking impression when I arrived at the castle of the Emir of Tatra.

I looked down on my left into a little gully. At the bottom was a clump of scrub and low lying trees. They would be sufficient to hide the women and provide shade. The women would also be able to scratch in the sandy ground until they found water.

We would lie up here for the rest of the day and for most of the night. This would ensure that the women were rested and looking their best when we arrived at the castle of the Emir of Tatra the following morning. It would also enable the slave drivers to practice their coffles in the prancing step that would be used as we approached the castle.

I gave a wave of my hand, and turning my horse began to ride down into the gully, followed in turn by the display team, the coffle of blond women, and the two coffles of matched pairs, together with their respective mounted Negro slave drivers and boy assistants.

In no time camp was being made, with a special tent for myself and another for the slave drivers and Matrak. The various coffles of women had started excavating a little pool of water with their hands and were then allowed to drink.

Each coffle was then chained down to stakes driven into the ground and to the trees. To protect herself from the cold night air, each girl was allowed to wrap herself in the thick horse blanket she carried rolled up on her back above her load.

Fires were lit, and soon Tulip brought a delicious meal to my tent. I saw a large pot of porridge being taken to the coffles and a large dollop being thrown down onto the ground before each woman.

My two stirrup girls had now been tied by their collar chains to a stake driven into the ground by the entrance to my tent. Unlike the other women, they were not given any food of their own. Instead they enjoyed the privilege of being given by Tulip the scraps left over on my plate. I could see them hungrily watching me as I ate.

Each day I had unlocked the two girls' neck chains from the stake in the ground outside my tent, and instead chained them to the central tent pole inside. Then periodically during the day, as I dozed, I snapped my fingers and lay back whilst they amused me with their tongues, their mouths and their now heavy breasts.

But increasingly I felt dissatisfied.

Here I was with two adoring pretty creatures competing with each other to satisfy me, and yet I was feeling unfulfilled, lonely and homesick.

All I could think of was that only a few yards away, outside the tent, lay a helpless, chained and most attractive young English woman of the same social background as myself. She was a young woman with whom I could have laughed and chatted in English and have forgotten all my loneliness - and yet she was taboo. She was not mine, she was the property of the Pasha and would soon belong to the Emir of Rebar. It was a situation I just could not stand a moment longer.

Angrily I called for Matrak.

When he arrived, I threw him the keys to the coffle chains.

I gave him an order. He blanched. Such was the power of the old Pasha. Matrak would, of course, eventually have to go back to Marsa with me, back to a port ruled by the Pasha.

I let him go away and rest. In this way he could, if necessary, say he was unaware of what happened. I told him to give the keys to Tulip. Tulip was my page boy. Probably in the eyes of the outside world he was a good deal more.

A little later I repeated the same order to Tulip. The encampment was now quiet, as the women slept. The slave drivers also slept, except for the guard on duty, and I had told Tulip to send him off to check that no one was approaching from down the gully.

Five minutes later I heard Tulip returning. I heard gasps from my stirrup girls chained outside the entrance to my tent like guard dogs. But it did not matter what they saw - they would not be returning to Marsa!

Tulip pulled aside the entrance flap of my tent. Behind him, led on a lead, was Henrietta!

Her eyes were wide with a mixture of fear and astonishment. I stood up and snapped my fingers. She fell to her knees and began to lick my boots. It was important to establish the correct relationship from the start.

I told Tulip to remain, holding her chain. He had after all frequently attended on me in my harem when I was dallying with a pretty girl. Without his presence, I did not think I could resist the temptation to raise Henrietta up and to kiss her hand as an equal. Without his restraining presence, I did not think that I could really treat such a beautiful and desirable fellow inhabitant of the British Isles as a mere slave.

I looked down and admired her long naked back. I admired her full breasts hanging down under her. I wondered what they would be like in milk. I wondered what her flat little belly would soon be like when the Emir forced her into her new role of brood mare. My loins stirred as these thoughts surged through my brain.

I could not help thinking how superior the Moslem religion and culture was to the Christian one, at least from a man's point of view. Good Christians would regard my behaviour to Henrietta as abhorrent, Moslems would regard it as the proper attitude of a man towards a slave girl. The latter certainly seemed, at that moment, more in line with a man's normal and natural feelings towards an attractive young woman whom he held in his power.

"Enough!" I suddenly said in English.

She raised her head and looked up at me, now with a mixture of fear and respect. It is moments like this that made the ownership of a pretty woman worth all the trouble and expense.

"Listen carefully," I continued in English. "This page boy does not understand a word of English - nor does anyone else here, not even Matrak your own slave driver. You and I can say what we like to each other, just as we did for a brief moment when the Pasha was making up his mind whether to buy you or not."

"That awful old man!" cried Henrietta bitterly.

"That virile old man," I corrected her with a laugh, "who deigned to take you into his harem, and whose slave you still are - for the time being."

"What do you mean: for the time being?" came the cultured voice that had so haunted my dreams for months.

"Stop asking questions and tell me about yourself," I ordered her. "I want to hear more about your life in England. I want to hear all about your friends, about your husband, about what they are saying in England now, about what clothes they are wearing, and who the Prince Regent is sleeping with - or at least who the gossips say he is sleeping with. Tell me everything you know!"

I lay back and closed my eyes. At last I would be able to hear an English woman telling me all about herself. It would be something I had not heard for many years. The fact that the woman was half naked, with her bare breasts trembling deliciously just in front of me was neither here nor there. She was not my property. My adoring stirrup girls could satisfy my manly needs later. For the time being I just wanted to listen to an attractive English woman talking to me of her life, her hopes and her fears. It was something that I had not experienced since leaving England.

CHAPTER 26 - I DISPOSE OF SOME FEMALE MERCHANDISE

I spurred my horse into a trot and led my line of coffled women into the castle of the Emir of Tatra.

We had made a brave sight as we approached the castle. Tulip rode ahead of me with a huge Turkish flag, my two stirrup slaves were holding up my ceremonial umbrellas, and more Turkish flags flew from poles held up by the harnesses of the prancing matched pairs, who were no longer, of course, carrying their heavy packs.

The bells attached to the wrists of the women were ringing loudly as they ran. I could also hear the cracking of the whips of the slave drivers and their boy assistants as they made sure that none of the women lagged, and that they all maintained perfect alignment. Their naked breasts bounced and swung in unison as they all ran in step together. Their freshly washed cutaway trousers prettily displayed their beauty lips. The display team and my stirrup girls, of course, also showed off their now well swollen bellies.

In the middle of all this ran the half naked coffle of future brood mares, their blond hair still covered by their chadors. I saw the brand of the Pasha on the belly of the leading girl. Henrietta! My heart leapt, but I knew I must control my feelings at this critical moment. I must not risk ruining the whole enterprise for a mere slave girl.

I saw a small crowd of dignitaries standing on the steps that surrounded the castle courtyard. Alerted to my arrival, they were eager to see the display. Their splendid robes contrasting with the half nakedness of the white girls running behind me.

I could see the men's astonishment as I led the cortage round the courtyard, still at a brisk trot, our flags flying, the matched pairs prancing along with their knees raised high, the display team thrusting their bellies forward, and the stirrup girls struggling to hold their ornamental parasols up over my head. Bells rang, whips cracked, both mixing with the loud admonishments of the slave drivers.

As I continued to circle the courtyard, I could see the faces of the spectators looking increasingly lascivious as they watched the highly erotic spectacle. The weeks of training in the fort were certainly paying off!

Some of the stern faced men pointed admiringly to the exposed lips of the display team. Others pointed to their swollen bellies. Some were pointing to my well trained stirrup girls. All were admiring the matched pairs, and the way each pair was driven on by the spiked metal balls hanging from the chain that linked each yoke to that of the pair behind them.

Finally I rode up to two particularly distinguished looking men, with long beards and hooked noses, standing in front of the rest. I had recognised the tall man, from Tulip's description, as being the Emir of Tatra. The rather cruel looking, short and fat man standing next to him ... was he ... he must be ... yes, it was the Emir of Rebar!

I had arrived at a most opportune moment. This was obviously a gathering of the tribes, probably to co-ordinate their treachery with the French.

I slipped off my horse, which my stirrup girls then held, and salaamed deeply. I heard a word of command from behind me. All the women fell to their knees and prostrated themselves, their foreheads touching the ground.

"Your Excellencies," I said, "in the name of Allah, the Merciful, the Compassionate, I greet you in the name of the Pasha of Marsa, and of my Master the Sultan, His Imperial Majesty, may the blessing of Allah be upon him."

I pointed to the coffles of kneeling women.

"I bring you presents in the name of the Sultan, may he live for ever."

There was a sudden outbreak of delighted chatter amongst the men. These women were presents! I could feel that I had the men in the palm of my hand. I must strike whilst the iron was hot. After pausing for greater effect, I continued.

"Our Holy Koran says: 'Beautiful for mankind is love of the passions that come from women'. So, the Pasha of Marsa sends you these gifts as a sign of his regard for you and for your manly and practical needs."

I paused again. I could see that they were all looking at me wonderingly.

"For His Highness the Emir of Tatra, these tall white women, pregnant to Dinka giants - for his cotton and coffee fields."

The first line of the display gracefully stood up, displaying themselves to the Emir. He looked astonished and yet delighted.

I turned to the short fat man, and held my breath for an instant.

"And for the breeding farm of the Emir of Rebar," - just a faint acknowledgement, obviously I was right - "for the distinguished Emir of Rebar, this group of a blond mother, with two blond daughters of breedable age and her uncut blond son."

He gasped in amazement as the three women and the boy rose and as the chadors of the women and the turban of the boy were removed by Matrak, letting their long hair cascade down. Only Henrietta remained kneeling, as previously ordered, her head to the ground and her hair still hidden by her chador.

"And, your Excellency, as you can see, the mother will shortly be presenting you with another blond child. It will be from the same sire. His Excellency, the Pasha, was most upset to hear of your loss of brood mares, and hopes that this modest little group will help quickly re-establish your breeding lines."

The Emir of Rebar was clearly overcome with amazement and delight. Never in his wildest dreams could he have ever imagined such a gift. I had already won over the two leaders.

"And to each of you, the Pasha sends a stirrup girl to run at your horse's side, and to present you soon with a strong Dinka mulatto Haratin slave."

At these words, my two stirrup girls jumped up. Matrak unfastened their collar chains from my stirrups and led the girls over to the smiling Emirs. Bowing, he handed the buxom Italian's chain to the Emir of Rebar and Beatriz's to the Emir of Tatra. I took a last sad glance at Beatriz as the girls stood behind their new Masters holding their parasols over their heads.

Then I turned to the other men, minor chieftains but still vital for safeguarding Barbary from the French.

"And for you, oh my brothers, your friend the Pasha of Marsa reminds you how our great Prophet Mohammed, may he always be blessed, has shown us by his own words and deeds how Allah has meant us to enjoy women. The Prophet of course married several women. But he also enjoyed a countless number of slaves. These are what I bring you in the name of our great and mighty Sultan, may he live for ever." I paused again for effect before speaking again slowly and deliberately so that all might understand. "For each of you, one of these pairs of matched slaves are for your private enjoyment - and to keep!"

At these words, the two coffles of yoked women rose. I could see the men looking at them eagerly, each deciding which pair he wanted most. My plan was indeed going well.

"Or for those who prefer a beautiful slave who is pregnant, he offers you one of these."

The team now stood up, creating even more excitement.

"As you will see," I went on, "these slaves are beautiful white women from Europe. Christian women snatched by our brave corsairs from the infidels, and brought here for the enjoyment and use of true believers. But they are only a foretaste of what the

Pasha will continue to send you, and what indeed you can buy for yourselves in the slave markets of Marsa. As the Prophet said: 'He who is able to enjoy women and does not do so for any reason is not of me and he has lost his earthly paradise'. Let us, my brothers, continue to enjoy an earthly paradise populated by such lovely women!"

These words had their desired effect. The men were calling out their agreement and turning to each other, nodding their heads.

"But, my brothers in Islam, we can only enjoy this happy state of affairs for so long as the hated Christians are kept out of our land, for no such slaves will exist if the infidels come."

I could see that the men were listening to me closely.

"Look at these women. Look at these slaves. They are for you! Did not our gracious Prophet also say: 'Blessed is the passionate women, responsive in copulation and blessed is the man who takes her and disciplines her'. My brothers, enjoy the gifts of that I bring you. You and the Sultan have a mutual interest in ensuring that the infidels are kept out of our land, so that the flow of such gifts can continue. But the Pasha wishes to warn you that the hated French, the evil men who have even killed their own King and his Queen, are even now planning to invade and seize this land!"

The two Emirs looked at me sharply, as did the other men. My words had clearly touched a nerve. The treacherous swine!

"You all know what desolation that evil man Napoleon Bonaparte brought about in Egypt before he was driven out. Now he is planning to try and make up for that defeat by seizing this land. If he does so, then he will strike down our religion, he will desecrate our holy place, he will introduce abominable Christian ways, he will abolish slavery and give so-called freedom to our slave girls and concubines. He will even forbid us our harems. Brothers, I say no! Never! Let us all unite behind the flags of the Sultan to fling the infidel back into the sea. Indeed, when he hears of our united resolve he will never dare invade."

My words were greeted enthusiastically.

"Come, my brothers, renew your allegiance to the Sultan, so that I can discuss with each of you in turn your rightful share of these gifts."

I went on in this vein for some time before turning to the Emir of Tatra and asking where the women could be locked up in safety

139

whilst we discussed their distribution. At the same time, I quietly told the Emir that the Pasha was concerned to provide him with a steady supply of tall strong white girls to breed intelligent tall mulattos for his cotton and coffee plantations.

The Emir smiled delightedly. He walked up to the front line of the display team, examining the frightened girls.

"Tell our friend, the Pasha of Marsa," he said in a loud tone, amidst general murmurs of assent, "that with gifts like these, he can remain sure of our loyalty and that we will proclaim it far and wide for all to hear - even the infidel French across the sea."

I could hardly believe my luck! It had all proved really quite easy.

Meanwhile the other men were crowding round the coffles of matched pairs, arguing amongst themselves as to which should have the first choice.

The Emir of Rebar was having a look at the Swedish family. Then he came back to me.

"The blessings of Allah on the Pasha," he cried. "I asked for his help after my sad losses, but I never expected to receive anything like this. They will save years of patient waiting and breeding."

The tall Emir of Tatra called for silence.

"My brothers," he said, "we are all overwhelmed by the generosity of the Pasha and must take his warning very seriously. Let us go indoors and discuss the matter further, whilst these women are put away in my stables."

I followed the Emir into the castle. We all sat down in the Emir's Majlis, his council chamber. All the talk was of how they could best unite in a show of force to frighten off the French. My mission was indeed accomplished.

Later, each leader received his allotted pair of yoked women, or his share of the display team. The Emir of Tatra's men took away his share of the display team. The Swedish family had been set aside for the Emir of Rebar.

It was later that day that the fat little Emir of Rebar sent for me. He was sitting cross-legged on a large cushion, behind him was standing a tall Negro. He came straight to the point in a very un-Eastern way.

"Why have you kept back the other blond girl?"

140

"I ... I ... did not feel that she was up to your standard of beauty, or suitable for breeding, Your Excellency," I stammered, caught unawares.

"Then why did you march her all the way here?" demanded the Emir. "She has the brand of the Pasha himself. He would not have sent her, if he did not feel that she was suitable for my breeding farm. He would know the importance of developing another line with whom this potentially magnificent Swedish line could be out-crossed."

These were arguments for which I simply had no answer. They were what I had been dreading all along.

"Let me be the judge of her suitability - together with my breeding overseer, Opala." He pointed to the young Negro standing behind him. "I have sent for him to take delivery of the Swedish family. Please send for the other girl and let him look at her too."

He smiled crookedly. "With her in my breeding pens, the Pasha could rest assured that my loyalty to the Sultan would be certain. If I have her, then I will immediately issue a call to the tribes to rally behind the Sultan and repudiate the French bribes."

It was the first time anyone had actually admitted being in touch with the French or that they were offering bribes. Clearly, I had no alternative but to send for Henrietta.

So it was that a few minutes later, Matrak led in a very frightened looking English woman. Her wrists were chained to the ring on the back of her collar, so that she could not interfere with her examination. She was still dressed just in her revealing trousers and I could feel my loins stirring at the sight.

She seemed astonished to see me. "Oh no, not you again!" she cried out, making me feel a complete swine.

Before she could say another word, Matrak lead her up to Opala, who bent and began to run his hands over her flat belly and breasts. Then he stood up and examined the roots of her hair, checking for signs of dyeing, checking that she really was a natural blond.

He stood up and nodded to the Emir. "Just what we need," he said.

My heart sank, Henrietta's fate was sealed.

For several days the Emirs and tribal leaders feasted, enjoyed their new women, and decided on what they should do to follow up the anti-French proclamation to which they had all affixed their names. Only I was left with nothing.

The breeding overseer of the Emir of Rebar had left immediately after he had inspected Henrietta, taking her and the Swedes, as if he could not wait another minute before getting them into his breeding pens.

I had sent the slave drivers back to Marsa. There was nothing more for them here. I would send Matrak back also, to report the success of the expedition to the Pasha, as soon as final details had been agreed. I did not want to draw attention to myself by travelling fast. I would return more slowly with Tulip.

Somehow, despite the initial elation of success, it now all seemed to be rather an anticlimax. I was beginning to loathe the fat smug Emir of Rebar, who had so completely out-manoeuvred me and was now the owner of Henrietta. I could hardly bear to think about what was happening to her. I just longed to get back to my harem, and to forget all about her in the eager arms of my concubines. However, I had to stay on to be able to tell the Pasha about the final arrangements.

Then suddenly the Emir gave me an unexpected invitation.

"I think you should come and see my breeding farm, so that you can tell the Pasha just how important his gifts have been - and how his gifts are settling down to their new life. It is only a short distance from here, up in the cool mountain air - and from there you can go straight on back to Marsa."

My heart almost stopped.

I did not know whether to be thrilled or appalled, but in any event I could not refuse what must have seemed to be both a courteous and sensible suggestion.

CHAPTER 27 - ESCAPE AND EVASION

Followed at a respectable distance by our entourage, in my case Matrak and Tulip, the Emir of Rebar and I rode up to the high wall surrounding the farm buildings. The entrance was well guarded, as one would have expected with such valuable creatures inside.

The Emir had been explaining that it had only been his main, long established, breeding lines that had been affected by the sudden illness that had swept through his breeding pens. Many of the blond women he had more recently acquired had survived. But in the normal way it would take him generations to re-establish a new breeding line that would stamp its look on the majority of the slaves the farm produced. That was why the entire Swedish family was such a windfall.

He, therefore, now planned to use the Swedish boy on many of his other women, as well as on his mother and sisters.

Opala, the Emir's breeding overseer, came out of his comfortable little hut to greet us as we entered the large building. Inside, it was like a stable but instead of loose boxes or stalls, there was a line of raised cages, facing a central passageway. There was a familiar stables-like smell.

The floors of the cages were covered with straw, except for a strip down the center of each cage which was cemented and kept bare. A channel ran down the strip of cement and under the bars at the front of the cage, so that any liquids would drain away into a gutter running down the side of the passageway.

We walked up and down inspecting the women in the cages and suddenly - there was Henrietta, peering at me through bars!

"Can we have a closer look at one of them?" I asked, attempting to be nonchalant. "How about that one?"

The Negro produced a key and unlocked the cage door. As he reached into the cage, Matrak, in his apparent eagerness, bumped into him.

The key fell to the ground and Matrak's uncharacteristically clumsy feet sent it spinning away, but he ran after it, an embarrassed back presented to us as he rubbed the dirt from it. Then he returned and handed it to his fellow eunuch with an apologetic little bow ...

... anxious time passed after that. It seemed like an age before at last we were out in the open and could speak freely.

"Well, Matrak?" I asked.

He looked at me proudly, then held up his hand and opened it.

There before my anxious eyes was a piece of clay with the imprint of a key in it!

"Is that a good enough impression?" I asked. "Are you sure you can make a proper key from it?"

He looked at me as if I was stupid. Of course he could do it!

"That easy," he said, with the widest grin I have ever seen.

My elation knew no bounds, but my military training took over.

"We must go over my plan in detail," I said.

So we did, and it was in good heart that we set up camp.

The moon had not yet risen when we slowly rode back to the farm that night. Tulip was ahead on foot, finding the way. Matrak was leading Tulip's horse. I was leading one of our pack horses. It would have to serve for Henrietta - although she had been brought up in the country, I doubted if she were an accomplished rider.

We would have two hours to rescue Henrietta and get away, before the moon rose and the guards might see us.

In the total darkness, we dismounted in a gully half a mile from the white walls. Leaving Tulip to hold the horses and keep them quiet, Matrak and I crept up to the farm.

Just as we had expected, there was little sign of the guards on this side of the farm. Security was slack, I thought. No one had ever dared to raid the breeding farm of the Emir of Rebar - nor was anyone expected to!

Then suddenly, just as we were about to throw a rope with a loop on the end up to a projection on top of the wall, we heard footsteps and voices from the top. We froze. The guards passed laughing and shouting at each other.

We waited in silence for another ten minutes. There was no more sign of the guards. I beckoned to Matrak. With his muscular torso, he should have no difficulty, I had reckoned, on throwing the rope up and snagging the top of the wall.

On his third attempt, the rope caught. Cautiously, one at a time, we climbed up. There was a narrow platform for patrolling guards at the top of the wall, and then a drop down again.

Leaving the rope in place, Matrak and I crept towards the farm building in which the women were housed. I had noticed that there was no door to the building - evidently the Emir relied more on his cages and the high wall rather than on doors - and the knowledge that there was nowhere for the women to go if they did escape.

Soon we were in the building. To prevent any of the sleeping women from suddenly crying out in alarm, Matrak played the part of one of their real black supervisors. Confidently he strode down the passageway, cloaked by the darkness, and I crept behind him. I stopped in front of Henrietta's cage whilst Matrak continued on down the passageway to distract attention.

"Henrietta!" I whispered. There was an answering gasp. "Keep quiet!"

I thrust the key Matrak had made into the lock of her cage. It would not turn!

Everything seemed lost. Then suddenly, as I wrestled with the key, the lock turned. I thrust open the door to the cage, grabbed Henrietta and pulled her out.

I closed the cage door, and locked it again. That might mislead a casual inspecting guard during the night.

Already Matrak was coming down the passageway again. I heard him trying the locks of several cages - like a real guard. We crept down behind him. Suddenly we were outside and running towards the wall and the rope.

Henrietta tried to say something. It sounded like an apology for having misjudged me.

"Not now!" I whispered urgently. "Not now! Just do what we say."

The march had toughened Henrietta up considerably. It took only a few minutes to get her up the rope and over the wall. But in the darkness, I thought we were never going to find Tulip and the horses. Suddenly I heard his whistle from behind us. We had overshot him!

Quickly Matrak and Tulip, dressed Henrietta as a page boy, and wound a turban round her head to hide her long blond hair.

Minutes later we were mounted and on our way.

We parted, Matrak and Tulip to go on ahead to Marsa to give the Pasha the good news of the Emir's conversion to our cause, Henrietta to come on more slowly with me - my personal garzon! No one would guess that under her clothes was the body of a most attractive woman, a woman for whom I had just risked my life!

Two more anxious days passed as we pressed on for home and safety.

Whilst I was planning Henrietta's rescue I had worried a lot about what would happen when the Emir discovered his loss, and whether or not he would pursue us. But nothing had happened -

145

probably he merely supposed that it had been Tuareg raiders. They had a reputation, after all, for being clever metal workers, especially with keys and locks. He would probably think they had become alarmed by something and had run off with the only woman they had got so far. In any case, I decided, he would never mention the matter. What a loss of face it would be to admit that a woman had been snatched from under his nose, from out of his precious breeding farm!

Anyway, there was no time for second thoughts now.

Since Henrietta was not used to riding, we had laid up the following day, hidden amongst the numerous gullies that scarred the undulating plain, and then ridden most of the following day and night to get as far away from the Emir's breeding farm as possible.

We had passed several caravans and groups of travellers. None had seemed interested in a lone Albanian merchant, travelling back to the coast with his garzon riding respectably behind him.

Now we sat at ease round the camp fire in front of my tent, with the horses picketed a few yards away, and Henrietta still dressed as my page boy.

"How unbelievably lucky I was to be rescued by an Englishman," she murmured, a hand on my knee. "Why, you might have been some awful Arab or Turk planning to put me in his harem!"

I smiled. Putting her in my harem was my greatest desire. In my harem! If only we could achieve it, but still it seemed an impossibility. She bore the Pasha's brand mark on her belly - how could I keep her from him?

I ran my eyes over her slim boyish figure and strong looking face yet again. I knew that I would try, whatever the danger.

And at that very moment, as I looked at my lovely page boy, I could feel my loins stirring. I wanted to enjoy more than her mere company.

"Why do you smile?" she asked petulantly. "There's nothing funny about being shut up in a man's harem, I can tell you!"

"I'm sorry. Yes, of course, it must be dreadful." I smiled innocently. How wonderful it would be to have her at my mercy in my harem. But could I ever really achieve this? Meanwhile, it really was very amusing to toy with her and pretend to treat her with the respect that she was used to enjoy from English men.

She looked up at me lovingly. "Oh how will my husband and I ever begin to thank you for my freedom!"

"Very simply," I replied with a laugh and reaching down took her into my arms.

"Oh! You are so attractive and masterly!" she cried, yielding her soft body to my embrace. Then I felt her stiffen. "But my husband! You can't expect me to deceive my husband now that I have been rescued."

Again I laughed. The little minx was trying to square her Christian conscience with her natural desires.

"I am an English gentleman, a former fellow officer of your husband. I do not ravish wives of fellow officers."

She laughed, reassured, but also perhaps a little disappointed. It was time, I felt, for matters to move forward.

"I may not be interested in Mrs. James Hamilton," I said firmly, "but I certainly am interested in my page boy. Mrs. James Hamilton's honour will not be sullied and her feminine charms will remain unentered. But it is time the page boy pleased his Master."

"Oh no! No!" cried Henrietta in genuine horror and disbelief, though doubtless the Pasha must have used her in this way and had his black eunuchs both prepare and train her accordingly. "No! Not that! You're an Englishman!"

I seized her wrists and pulled off her page boy's blouse. Her breasts were still tightly bound. Let them remain so! It would heighten the effect and make what I was now going to do all the more realistic.

I reached for my riding whip. I saw Henrietta give a little start.

"Now the boy will start to please his Master, and do not pretend you do not know what I mean - if you want to avoid the whip."

With a sob, she lowered her hands. Soon they were busy with the buttons of my breeches. I felt the tips of her fingers. Again I raised the whip. This time, within seconds, and with another sob, she had lowered her head.

I lay back, the whip still in my hand. The once sheltered and coy vicar's daughter had been well trained in the Pasha's harem. It was interesting how the mere mention and sight of the whip was enough to make her switch from being the gracious Mrs. James Hamilton to being a mere terrified slut of a slave girl.

My pleasure was intense. Thanks to the occasional menacing movement of my whip it was also prolonged. The black eunuchs had taught her that the object was not to bring her Master quickly to a climax, but rather to see how long he could be kept in a highly aroused state. 'Do not let the pot boil over if you wish to enjoy the most delicious food,' is an old Turkish saying, 'but rather keep it simmering.'

But I was on dangerous ground. In Turkish law, Henrietta still belonged to the Pasha.

CHAPTER 28 - FACE TO FACE WITH THE PASHA

"Halt! - or I shoot!"

The order came from the sergeant in charge of a detachment of the Pasha's own Black Guards manning a road block a few miles out of Marsa.

It was the detachment that had guarded the fort whilst the slave girls were being got fit for the march. They had recognised me, despite my disguise as an Albanian merchant. Perhaps that was why these particular troops had been sent.

"We have orders to take you and your garzon to the Pasha immediately," said the sergeant.

Taken to the Pasha! My heart was in my mouth. Was I already under arrest? The very fact that they were expecting a garzon to be with me boded ill.

The sergeant ordered his men to form up around Henrietta and I, and sent off one man on horseback to Marsa. To alert the Pasha, of my arrival? Was the escort to take me to prison? It hardly looked like a ceremonial sign of welcome.

In silence, we passed through the market gardens and small farms that surround Marsa. Half naked white women, mixed with mulatto Haratin women, often chained together in pairs or working in chain gangs, were busy hoeing, or straining to pull a plough or harrow, or running round and round as they pulled or pushed a long bar that turned a water wheel to irrigate the fertile land. Negro overseers, dressed in brilliant coloured baggy Shalwar and carrying long carriage whips, strode importantly up and down, ensuring that the women were kept hard at work.

148

We approached the city walls with its rows of rotting heads displayed on spikes. Perhaps my head would be amongst them tomorrow!

We passed through the City gates, manned as usual by Black Guards - for my Janissaries did not demean themselves by carrying out routine guard duty. Immediately we were in a maze of filthy, narrow, dusty, twisting lanes. Donkeys carrying merchants and farmers, or loads of merchandise, brushed past me. The stench was appalling. Running along barefooted in the filth behind many of the donkeys were slave girls covered with white or black shrouds with only a little cotton grill to look through. Their wrists were often chained to the donkey's saddle. Veiled women stood in the doorways calling out to each other and contemptuously pointing to the passing slave women.

We came to an open square dominated by the large white painted palace of the Pasha. It served as an administration center, as well as housing his large harem and reception rooms - and, of course, down below, the dungeons. Were they my destination?

The large heavy gates swung open, and closed behind me. We were now in a small courtyard. There standing on the steps that led down from his Majlis, or meeting chamber, was the Pasha.

His face was a mask.

I looked round. The courtyard was lined with more Black Guards, sabers drawn.

I quickly dismounted and signalled to Henrietta to do the same. I salaamed deeply, kneeling on the cobbles, desperately hoping to save my skin. Out of the corner of my eye I saw that Henrietta had flung herself down with her forehead to the ground in a gesture that was more typical of a well trained slave girl than the garzon she was supposed to be.

"So you have got yourself another pretty garzon out of all this!" said the Pasha. "I did not know you were partial to white eunuch boys, though it is a taste that I approve of - in moderation. Let's have a good look and see if I share your enthusiasm in this case."

My heart sank again as I heard him give an order. Three Black Guards, huge Negroes each of them, marched forward and seized Henrietta. They dragged her up in front of the Pasha. One held her wrists behind her back, another clasped her mouth tightly shut so that she could not cry out, the third pulled her Shalwar down to her knees.

With sickening dismay I realised that her hairless beauty lips would now be on display. And, even worse, if the turban on her head had perhaps temporarily disguised her identity, it would now be only too evident from the brilliant green brand on her belly.

The Pasha's brand! He looked closely at her, but said nothing.

Henrietta's eyes were almost bursting out of their sockets with sheer terror. Mine must have looked similar, as I realised that the game was indeed up.

The Pasha gave another order. Sickened, I saw the Negroes turn Henrietta round, the Shalwar round her knees making it awkward for her.

The Pasha would now be looking at the Emir of Rebar's breeding number tattooed on her buttocks. Had the Emir sent word to the Pasha, asking him to look for a girl tattooed with that number? Had he asked for my head, carefully salted in the Moorish way, to be sent to him?

There was a long pause. I would give a good account of myself with my short scimitar, but the end would never be in doubt. It would make a fine, if short spectacle. Probably that was why the Pasha had received me standing on the steps of the courtyard rather than inside his palace. Was I about to be slain like a gladiator in the Roman arena - and for the amusement of the Pasha? Where, oh where, were my own Janissaries?

Then the Pasha laughed aloud.

"With your new larger harem quarters waiting to be filled," he said, "I am surprised that you waste time dressing a slave girl up as a boy."

My heart was in my mouth! But what did he mean? What new harem quarters?

"I would have thought," he added dryly, "that you would prefer to dress a lovely creature like that as a half naked houri, an eager concubine. Perhaps you don't deserve her. Perhaps I should ..."

He was smiling now, as if enjoying some private joke.

I looked up at him in astonishment.

"Excellency! I do not understand. What new larger harem quarters?"

Again he laughed.

"Don't you know?" he said teasingly. "Abdul Rahman Bey has been recalled by the Sublime Porte to Constantinople. I had something to do with that! Anyway he has sold off his harem and gone. I have issued a firman promoting you to his position, and to his palace - Hussein Bey. Now get up off your knees, it is undignified for a Bey!"

I staggered to my feet, completely overcome. Me! A Bey!

The Pasha came down the steps. Quickly that kind, cruel, old man took me in his arms and embraced me.

"You have done well, my son. Matrak has told me all. You owe him a great deal. Now go to your new palace and enjoy the women of your harem in their new quarters. They are eagerly awaiting your return - even if they are at present still so few that they rattle around it like half a dozen peas in a coconut shell."

Speechless, I just stood listening to him as he went on.

"And do hurry up and take that ... boy ... that girl ... out of my sight before I change my mind ..."

I bowed and turned to go.

"Return tomorrow morning. I want to brief you about going to Malta to see the British authorities. They'll believe you now, if you tell them of your adventures."

Malta! I thought. But my thoughts were interrupted by another loud laugh from the Pasha.

"But you'd better not tell them about your latest acquisition - that garzon! I don't want your mission being wrecked by any disclosure of the whereabouts of a certain Mrs. James Hamilton."

"Yes, of course," I replied, my mind in a daze.

"No don't go out through that gate," cried the Pasha as I remounted. "Use this one."

He pointed to a closed gateway that led I knew into another, much larger courtyard. Two Black Guards pulled open the gate. I rode through it, to be greeted by a roar.

There, lined up on parade and looking immaculate, were my Janissaries. What they must have thought of me, dressed as I was as an Albanian merchant, and followed by a pretty garzon, is something I shall never know.

"Greetings to our Commander, Hussein Bey," they were shouting in unison. "Hussein Bey! Hussein Bey!"

As they formed up around me, to escort me to my new palace, I glanced back at Henrietta. She was just looking stunned by it all. Not speaking Turkish, she would not have understood a word.

CHAPTER 29 - I ENJOY A CERTAIN NEW SLAVE GIRL

Half an hour later, I was striding through my new domain - the palace of the Commander of the Janissaries. It was indeed a fine and luxurious building - a cross between the Turkish and Arab styles with ornate Arabesque tracery work over the windows, marble floors, tiled walls and high curved ceilings with a plethora of patios and tinkling fountains. It was also well endowed with screens from which one could look down into the harem, with its Turkish bath and small swimming pools.

Henrietta, still dressed as a boy, was running behind me as I strode through the beautiful rooms. She kept trying to speak to me, but I paid no attention. Finally we came to a corridor with a large iron barred door at the end of it.

Matrak and Abdul stood waiting for me, their eyes raised quizzically as they watched Henrietta trying to attract my attention.

"Everything is ready, Hussein Bey," reported Matrak with a bow.

I turned to Henrietta.

"Go with Matrak," I said briefly.

He led her towards the large door.

Suddenly she tried to break away from his grasp.

"Isn't that the door to a harem?" she cried.

"Indeed," I said.

"You mean to say that you have a harem! I can't believe it!"

"You will when you are safely locked up in it," I laughed, "though you will find that I only have a modest number of girls by comparison with the Pasha - at least so far."

"What!" she screamed. "You aren't really thinking of putting me into your harem!"

I said nothing.

"Oh no! No! You rescued me just to put me into your harem! But what about all the talk of sending me back to my husband?"

"That was your talk, not mine," I replied, beginning to get annoyed. "Now go along with Matrak and Abdul - and start your training as one of my concubines."

"No! No! Never! You can't do this to me. You're an Englishman!"

I signalled to Matrak. With a quick movement he picked Henrietta up in his strong arms. She was kicking and struggling, and beating her small fists against his huge chest. But he held her quite helpless, and was laughing as he did so. He enjoyed taming intransigent white women.

Abdul unlocked the large door.

"You swine! You unutterable swine! I hate you! I hate you!"

They were the last words I heard before the door to my harem closed on her, silencing her screams of protest.

Ten days passed and the eve of my departure for Malta as the Pasha's special envoy arrived. I had been busy briefing myself on just what to say to the British authorities, but I had also been enjoying the delights of my harem after my prolonged absence.

I had not yet sent for Henrietta. Matrak had advised me to leave her to him for the time being. I understood that his cane had been kept pretty busy, but that she had now settled down.

It was the siesta hour and I climbed into bed, thrusting my feet wide apart down under the bed clothes. As usual I heard the rattle of a chain beneath the bedclothes and idly wondered which girl Matrak had selected to perform on the short chain during my siesta.

Suddenly I realised that I was being caressed not by one little tongue, but by two. How charming. How clever of Matrak to provide two short chain girls on my last day.

Through the narrow Arab style fluted windows I could see out on the bay. It was not as calm nor as blue as it was in summer, but it was still a most attractive sight. Better than the grey old Thames at Westminster!

A beautiful small galley, a galliot, was racing across the waters. It was, I knew, the one that I had inherited from Abdul Rahman Bey. I enjoyed seeing my own female galley slaves being exercised in the afternoon as I took my siesta. It gave one a feeling of power - just as did the two girls tied down on their short chains below the bed covers.

The tickling under the bed clothes was getting more and more insistent. Having two girls, each striving to out-perform the other, was certainly an excellent idea.

I raised the bed covers and looked down. Two faces peered up at me, with the usual look of adoration. They were coupled together by a short chain that linked their shining collars. To the left was a dark eyed, dark haired beauty. It was a delightful sight. But I was even more delighted to see that the girl to the right was blue eyed and her hair was golden. Her tongue was also assiduously working away, up and down and to and fro, as she too strained to give me pleasure.

Etta and Henrietta!

They made a fine contrasting pair. I would tell Matrak also to train them to perform together in other ways for my amusement and to have them ready for my return. It would be something to look forward to. Such performances done in time to music needed to be well planned and rehearsed. The performers usually also needed a considerable application of their trainers whip before they were perfect. It would of course be desperately embarrassing for them both to be trained to put on such an intimate performance by a Negro.

However, it was indeed an indication of the effectiveness of Matrak's technique that he should so quickly have transformed, anyway outwardly, a resentful and angry Englishwoman into a well behaved young slave girl. Coupling them together by the neck was a stroke of genius. It made each strive to out-perform the other.

As I would be leaving for Malta the following day, I had planned to have a party in the harem that night. The girls would dance for my entertainment. But I did not feel that my enjoyment would be unduly upset by a little relief now. It would be amusing now to try both Etta and Henrietta out on a long chain. They had both performed well on the short chain.

I pulled the bell cord by the bed.

Abdul, my young black eunuch, was usually on duty in the afternoons and it was he who silently slid into my bedroom. I gestured with my hand. I saw him remove a key from his pocket.

He reached down and unfastened each girl's brass collar from the short chain that held them down to the bottom of the bed. Then he left as silently as he had entered.

Moments later I felt two slim forms sliding up on either side of me as I lay back, my hands clasped behind my neck. Two lovely little creatures reached up, each licking one side of my neck.

This was the life for a real man, I decided. Who would ever want to go back to England!

"Oh, Master!" whispered Etta adoringly in Lingua Franca.

"Oh, darling!" whispered Henrietta adoringly in English.

And to think that another six lovely creatures would be sitting in the harem, under the supervision of Abdul, each jealously wondering what was going on in my bed, and each determined to catch my eye at the party that night.

It was a stimulating thought.

Suddenly I flung Henrietta down on the bed. With a snap of my fingers I motioned to Etta to kneel behind me and continue her ministrations.

"Oh! Oh!" cried Henrietta as at last, after all these months, I enjoyed her for the first time as a woman - an unbelievably desirable woman who was looking up at me with adoring glazed eyes, as if I was God. I would show her that on the contrary I was her very human, if demanding, Master.

CHAPTER 30 - A FINAL SURPRISE.

I looked down through the wooden screen on the front of the balcony, down into the lit-up harem room at my six beautiful European women: quick tempered Francesca from Naples, little Etta from Sardinia, the exquisite Marie from France, the proud Carmen from Spain, the tall Paula from Greece, and, of course, Henrietta herself.

A feeling of pride and power surged through me. They all belonged to me. They were my slaves, to play with and do with as I liked.

They had all been resentful when they were first put into my harem. Some had even hated me at first. But now, in their different ways, they all loved me. How clever the Harem system was! It ensured that even an educated woman's natural sensuality was directed towards one man by making sure she had no contact with any others - and by making sure that she had no opportunity to direct this same sensuality towards her companions - or herself. The black eunuchs kept her outwardly as pure as the driven snow, whilst inwardly. thanks to the sensuous atmosphere of the harem, she remained frustrated and jealous, her nerves on edge, about to boil over at any instant - like a chained cheetah!

All six were wearing magnificent muslin evening dresses cut in the latest Parisian high waisted fashion, and were carrying fans and had tiaras in their now elaborately ringleted hair. Their collars had been removed, so that there was nothing to show that they were slaves as they walked gracefully up and down chatting like young girls eagerly awaiting the start of a their first ball.

It was Matrak who had obtained the dresses from a captured ship and suggested this ball - to be held on the eve of my departure for Malta. He had even found some musicians who could play a tolerable imitation of a romantic Viennese waltz.

I myself would wear my black evening coat with its high stiff velvet collar - one of the few remnants of my life in London as a young Guards officer, before having to flee the country after being found in bed with one of the Queen's Maids of Honour - found by the outraged Queen herself!

The question of other dancing partners for the gorgeously dressed women had been easily solved. Naturally there was no question of inviting other men to the ball. I could not possibly have allowed them to see my women unveiled and even if they had been veiled, the mere sight of these other men might have disrupted the strict harem discipline that Matrak enforced. In any case none of my Arab or Turkish friends knew how to waltz!

Tulip, however, came from a well known, if poor, Italian family. He might now be a rather feminised youth, but he certainly knew how to waltz. So did Jasmine, my young Italian harem hairdresser - also, of course a eunuch. The same ship that had carried the crate of women's dresses had also carried a crate of men's clothes, so it had been easy to dress them as outwardly foppish young European men of fashion. It had also not been difficult for Matrak to borrow good looking white eunuch youths belonging to other leading citizens of Marsa and to dress them, too, as dancing partners for my women.

156

I had wondered what to do about my two delightful Berber girls, Lala and Muneerah, who could hardly succeed as French women of fashion. Matrak had suggested that they should act as native servant girls, offering trays of drinks and little confections. At first I objected, not wanting to demean them in the eyes of my white women, but then I remembered their moment of triumph when I had humbled my European women by choosing both my Berber girls for my bed on my return. It would not matter now turning the tables on them for an evening ...

I stepped down the elaborate staircase to the spacious marble-floored receiving room. As I did so, five well dressed young men, perhaps rather effeminate looking young men, bowed to me in the European way. Smiling, I returned their bows. I made my way over to a large arm chair - another find from a captured ship and set like a raised throne in the corner of the room.

Sitting down, I clapped my hands. Instantly Lala and Muneerah, in long Arab caftan dresses, ran into the room carrying trays of captured Tuscany wine - not all the Prophet's followers always looked askance at a glass of wine, anyway on a special occasion!

Again I clapped my hands. The musicians, hidden away in an adjoining room so that they would not see my unveiled women, struck up. The atmosphere seemed perfect. I nodded at Matrak. He would soon disappear from sight so as not to spoil the effect of freedom for my women - whilst remaining discreetly nearby, ready to intervene with his cane at the slightest need.

Now however he opened a heavy iron-studded door - the normally well guarded door that led from the harem.

One by one, at first nervously tip-toeing and peering around unbelievably, and then with increasing confidence and an assumed air of nonchalance, the six gorgeous white women, beautifully dressed and groomed, came into the room.

I rose to my feet. One by one, each woman, keeping her eyes coyly down, came over and curtseyed deeply to me, slowly and elaborately. Then she stepped back, was offered a glass of wine and started to chat with the young 'men' that I had produced for them.

After a few unaccustomed sips of wine, and overcome by the romantic strains of music, they began to peer coquettishly up at me over the tops of their fans - just like girls at their first ball eyeing a handsome stranger.

As I came down from my chair Muneerah hurried forward with a tray of wine and Lala did the same with a tray of sweetmeats. Their eyes were lowered respectfully as they offered their trays. There was a sudden break in the conversation, as the women turned eagerly towards me.

"Please, ladies, do carry on," I insisted with a smile. I went over to Paula, my Greek girl. "You are looking positively radiant. May I ask you to dance?"

She blushed with pleasure as she slid into my arms. The other women looked on jealously as they resumed their conversations with the young men.

"Come!" I cried out. "I don't want to be the only one dancing."

Soon there were five other couples dancing round and round. But I could see that the women were not looking at their partners with love-lost eyes. They knew they had been rendered harmless. Instead they kept glancing at me.

For the next hour I danced and flirted with each in turn: I found all of them fascinating. Each looked up at me with adoration and love - and none more so than Mrs James Hamilton, now my branded slave Henrietta. She was mine now, all mine - even if the brand on her belly, like that on Carmen's, was that of the Pasha.

Indeed, I could not help thinking that giving away an attractive concubine as a way of rewarding a loyal henchman was indeed a clever idea of the Pasha's. I was reflecting on this as I stood watching the other dancers for a moment when suddenly Matrak slipped silently but unusually swiftly into the room and touched my arm.

"Your Highness," he said urgently, in a strained voice, "the Pasha is here!"

The Pasha! Utter disaster! I turned round frantically, intending to wave the women back behind the Harem door, the musicians into silence, and the wine glasses out of sight.

But I was too late. Striding into the room came the large and purposeful figure of the Pasha himself, and the music came to a ragged stop as the Pasha spoke.

"So this how our loyal Bey celebrates his ennoblement! With a European dance! With so called men dancing with unveiled women dressed as Christian houris! And not in the privacy of the harem, but here out in the Selamlik, the man's quarters! ... And serving wine!"

"Your Excellency, I ... I ..." I stammered, trying to seek an explanation of something that must seem quite unforgivable. I now saw that that following him were two huge black eunuchs, dressed in the Pasha's livery and each holding a chain fastened to one of the wrists of a totally invisible black shrouded figure.

"But don't let me upset your festivities," continued the Pasha, smiling now. "I just wanted to give you a surprise before you left for Malta."

"Your Excellency is too kind ..." I murmured, still desperately embarrassed.

The Pasha gestured to the black eunuchs. Whilst one of them held the mysterious woman's chained wrists behind her back, the other slowly began to unbutton the bottom of the front of her black shroud.

Suddenly the negro pulled it apart, disclosing her naked legs. Then slowly he pulled it further apart displaying her prominent and hairless beauty lips, with two little holes for an infibulation ring.

"Your Excellency, what ...?" I started to stammer, but the Pasha interrupted me.

"The Emir of Tatra was so overcome by my generosity in sending him all those white women, and in forgiving him for his disloyalty, that he sent back the most beautiful of the women to me as a sign of his renewed allegiance to the Sultan. As you originally chose her, I thought you might like to see her for yourself. She has proved to be a shrewd buy." He laughed. "I find her most enjoyable."My mind was racing.

The Pasha gestured to the black eunuchs. Again one held her hands helpless, whilst the other busied himself with the buttons of her shroud and veil. Slowly he began to lift it off her head. The young woman's pregnant body was gradually and erotically disclosed.

With a final jerk of the material he bared her face and head.

"I thought you might recognise her?" said the Pasha.

I did indeed! It was my stirrup girl from the march, Beatriz, the Portuguese Captain's young wife, the girl I had so wanted to buy for own harem.

"Your Excellency," I said, feeling rather mystified, "may I congratulate you on your acquisition of this fine new concubine?"

"No, no, you fool! She's yours!"

"But ... but, Your Excellency ... surely ..."

"You have others here whom I have also enjoyed." He pointed at the prostrate Carmen and Henrietta. "As to this one, she calls out your name even when sleeping in my bed. I cannot have that! It would be bad for harem discipline. Let her call out your name in her dreams in your harem!"

"Your Excellency! You are too kind! She is a wonderful present! Indeed a surprise! I do not know how to thank you ..."

The Pasha, that wily old man, smiled as he turned to go and his black eunuchs handed Beatriz's wrist chains to Matrak. "My son," he said, stopping by the door, "a word of advice from one well experienced in the ways of European women. Before you leave for Malta tomorrow, impress on her the fact of her new ownership. Then like the rest of your women, she will be crying for your quick return."

I heard Henrietta give a little cough, but I did not care. Henrietta was in my harem now, and would have to learn that I did not have favourites. She was very attractive it was true, and I adored her, but she was now just one of one of my women. I had indeed enjoyed her for my siesta earlier that day. But it would be Beatriz who would be in my bed later that night.

"Take her away and prepare her," I said to Matrak. He led her away, followed by the jealous looks of the other women.

"Now let the ball continues!" I cried. "Mrs Hamilton! I think the next dance is mine!"

For a moment, she looked at me with anger and hatred - but then submissively slipped into my arms, a picture of love and obedience.

Oh, the sheer joy of the harem system - and its effect on women!

Printed in Great Britain
by Amazon

55709975R00092